Safe Harbor

by

Jennifer Moore

The Lobster Cove Series

Safe Harbor

Cover Art by *Tina Lynn Stout*

The Wild Rose Press, Inc.
PO Box 708
Adams Basin, NY 14410-0708
Visit us at www.thewildrosepress.com

Publishing History
First Sweetheart Rose Edition, 2016
Digital ISBN 978-1-5092-0917-0
Print ISBN 978-1-5092-0970-5

The Lobster Cove Series
Published in the United States of America

Dedication

For Frank,
the Red Warrior

Chapter One

Dr. Seth Goodwyn stepped into the cool night air, grateful his paperwork was finally caught up and he could go home. He closed the clinic's glass door behind him, tugged to make sure it locked, and walked through the parking lot, fishing the keys from the pocket of his khakis. He put his laptop bag into the back seat and closed the door. Out of habit, he glanced up First Street, past the hospital to where he could just see the darkened windows of Sang Freud Coffee House in the glow of the streetlights.

Every morning, whether he was scheduled to work or not, he stopped in at Sang Freud's for an Americano with cream. But the outstanding coffee wasn't what brought him back time and again, nor was the friendly banter with Carlos Young, the coffee house owner. Rather, a particular strawberry-blonde barista, Melanie Owen had hijacked his thoughts.

He swung his gaze through the park and to Murphy's Bar on the cross-street, Oak Avenue. Or more specifically, the windows on the second floor where Melanie lived.

He squinted, tipping his head as a shadow moved in front of the upper window. *Is she awake this late?* Clicking the fob, he locked the car and slipped his keys back into his pocket. Maybe Melanie was on her way out. Headed down to the bar?

1

After stepping over the curb, he continued on the sidewalk in the direction of Murphy's, one of the few places still open at this hour. The small community of Lobster Cove did not exactly have a thriving night life. The quiet and the charming atmosphere were what had drawn him to this town on the Maine coast in the first place.

The possibility of having an actual conversation with Melanie, instead of the polite, brief exchanges he both dreaded and anticipated, sped his heart rate.

The petty dialog was not a result of Seth's lack of trying. He thought every morning of something witty to say that might elicit more than Melanie's typical one-word response. But for weeks, he'd left with a warm cup of coffee, a chocolate chip muffin, and a jaw tightened in frustration.

Still, his hope of an encounter with Melanie drove him onward. Since he first saw her a few weeks earlier, Seth had felt drawn to the woman. He and every other single man in town. Catching the gorgeous barista's attention had become an unspoken contest among Lobster Cove's bachelor population, but her disinterest caused most of their efforts to wane.

Seth didn't need a psychiatrist to tell him why he continued to obsess over her. Melanie was shy, almost secretive. She hardly met anyone's gaze directly and dodged personal questions about herself. The way her gaze darted to the coffee house door each time it opened and then relaxed once she saw who entered were all symptoms of a woman with a past. Melanie was afraid of something—or more likely, someone.

And Seth was a fixer. His need to take care of people, to save them, was the original reason he went into medicine. Not that he wanted to delve too deeply into the underlying issues behind his hero complex. Some things were simply too painful to deal with.

If only he could earn Melanie's trust, he would take care of her. He could protect her from whomever she was afraid of; he'd find out what she was hiding from.

Seth stopped at the corner of the bar and glanced up at the apartment's open window. A breeze fluttered the light curtain, and a shadow moved again. Irritated with himself, he blew out a huff of air and turned to go. *What am I doing? Standing in the street in the middle of the night? Staring at a woman's window like a weird stalker?*

A cry of pain sounded from inside the apartment.

Seth recognized Melanie's voice and whirled.

The shadow behind the curtain moved quickly this time. "Stop!" she screamed. "No! No! No! Stop!"

He bolted into the alleyway between the buildings and up the metal stairs. When he reached the landing, he tried the door, but it was locked.

Another cry of "No!" gave him the jolt of adrenaline he needed to kick near the doorknob, splintering the frame. Seth pushed open the door, breaking off chunks of wood as he burst into the room.

Melanie screamed again.

The apartment was lit dimly by a small television set.

Seth slid his hand up the wall and flipped on the light. He glanced around for a weapon and grabbed an umbrella from a nearby hook. With his pulse pounding in his ears, he swept his gaze around the room.

Melanie cowered in the corner of the couch, holding a throw pillow in front of her.

A small kitchen area was to his left, and directly in front of him was the living room. The attacker must be hiding. "Where is he?" Seeing her wide frightened eyes fueled another burst of energy. He bounded toward her, peering behind the couch.

With a gasp, she scrambled over the arm of the couch, pressing herself down into the little space next to the wall. "I'm calling the police!"

Good. Seth nodded and turned to the two darkened doorways. His heart raced. He shoved open one door, hoping to catch the attacker off guard, and then flipped on the light, revealing a small bathroom. Peering behind the door and batting aside the shower curtain revealed nobody, and he turned his attention to the other doorway.

He held onto the knob, his breath coming fast and his hands quivering. Was the attacker armed? Behind him, he could hear Melanie's voice.

"...broke into my apartment...yes...Dr. Goodwyn..."

Luckily, he had arrived when he did. He shoved the door then burst into the room, fumbling for the light switch. He looked behind the bed and whipped open the closet door, but Melanie's attacker was nowhere to be seen. Seth moved to the open window and stuck out his head, but he couldn't see anyone in the alley below. Relief poured over him, and his muscles eased as he returned to the living room.

Melanie had climbed back from behind the couch and was pressed against the wall behind the TV, moving in the direction of the front door. She held the phone to her ear.

Seth rounded the couch. "Melanie."

At the sound of his voice, she flinched and moved faster, stumbling over the cords. She glanced back at him with wide eyes and pulled her brows together tightly, making furrows above her nose. "Yes, he's still here," she said into the phone.

Seth shook his head. "No, he's gone now." He moved to intercept her, wanting to comfort her now that the danger had passed.

She cringed back, her gaze moving past him to the door. She squinted a bit but didn't relax her stance. "Who?"

"Your attacker must have climbed out of the window."

"My attacker?" She squinted tighter. "You…"

For a horrible second Seth froze. His thoughts stilled then raced at unbelievable speed as the reality of the situation crashed over him. Was there no intruder? Had she been alone? He glanced at the umbrella in his hand and then to the broken doorframe. *I'm the attacker.* He shook his head. "But you screamed. I heard you. You were screaming for someone to stop." He pushed the words through his dry throat.

A flush crept over her cheeks. She motioned toward the television. "I guess I was caught up in the game."

Seth's emotions somersaulted as his horror at what he'd done was infused with amusement. "You were screaming over a baseball game?"

"The first baseman missed the ball in the pickoff play." She shrugged and dropped her gaze with a soft smile.

Seth squinted at the TV. A laugh bubbled up in his chest. "Don't tell me you're a Yankee's fan."

Her shoulders were still tensed, but the terror was

gone from her face. "The man who broke into my apartment really shouldn't be pointing fingers."

Seth reached a hand toward her. Maybe she needed to sit down. "I'm sorry, I really thought—" He bit back a groan. What must she think of him? And what would happen when word got out that the town's doctor had broken into a woman's apartment?

The sound of the door creaking open made them both turn.

"Lobster Cove P. D." Officer Harris stood in the doorway, his hand resting on the gun at his waist.

Melanie glanced down at the phone she still held.

The officer motioned with a jerk of his head. "Doc, step away from the lady."

Seth's stomach dropped. "There's been a mistake, Nate. I thought—"

"Put down the umbrella and step away." Nate Harris's typically friendly brown eyes were dark and serious.

Seth dropped the umbrella and held up his hands. Sweat broke out over his forehead.

"You been drinking tonight, Doc?"

"No, it's nothing like that. Let me explain."

"Explain down at the station." Nate pulled the cuffs from his belt and stepped toward Seth. "You hurt, miss?"

"No. He didn't hurt me, Officer." Melanie moved away from the wall and folded her arms. "I think he was trying to protect me." She glanced up at Seth.

He nodded, warmth spreading from his chest at her shy smile.

Nate glanced back and forth between the two then bent his head to the side and spoke into the mike on his shoulder. He listened, his expression changing from stern to confused, and finally softening into a smirk. "Dispatch heard everything. You busted in here, guns blazing to rescue a woman yelling at a baseball game?" As he rested his forearm on the butt of his gun, he laughed. "Well, that's definitely a first." His stance relaxed. "I take it you're not pressing charges, Miss Owen."

Melanie shook her head then smiled at Seth.

A genuine grin with a little added sass. Not just a polite smile, but an expression of camaraderie at their shared experience—strange as it was. He grinned back. He hadn't only broken through her door, but through the barrier she used to distance herself from people. Some of her shyness was gone. She even held his gaze without looking away immediately. Maybe his screw up hadn't been a complete disaster.

Nate glanced at the game on the TV. "Stupid Yankees deserved that loss tonight."

Melanie blew out a breath and turned off the game. Frowning, she tossed the remote onto the couch. "Thanks a lot," she muttered. "A broken door, and now you ruined the game I recorded."

"Welcome to Red Sox country, Miss Owen." Seth held out a hand.

She shook it, raising a brow. "Maybe I will press charges after all."

Her expression brought a smile to his face. She still spoke softly, and her shy nature was apparent, but he felt as though he'd scored a victory, making her laugh, seeing her smile, and being at the receiving end of her teasing.

"Long as I've still got my cuffs handy, I should

arrest you for owning a teddy bear wearing a Jeter jersey." Nate motioned with his chin toward the couch. "That's just an offense against decency."

Seth liked Nate Harris, but he thought the officer's banter was moving from good-natured teasing to outright flirting. And the idea bothered him. "Thanks for coming so quickly, Nate." He held out a hand to shake.

The corner of Nate's mouth ticked, but he shook Seth's hand. "Next time, let the police do our job." He turned to Melanie. "If you need anything at all, you know where to find me."

"Thank you." Melanie ducked her head.

"I'll leave you two to sort this out." He flicked his hand toward the door frame as he left.

Seth glanced at Melanie and then walked to the door. "Wow, it really is broken. I didn't realize I was so manly."

Melanie rubbed her arms. "Thank you, Doctor. For what you did—even though you didn't need to. The effort...I appreciate it."

Her shyness had returned, and he wondered if it was because they were alone. He pulled at the splintered wood, breaking off a chunk. "Listen, I can't leave you here alone without a way to lock your door. You could sleep in my guest room tonight, and I'll get this fixed tomorrow."

Her gaze darted to his and then away. She wrapped her arms tighter, shaking her head. "I don't think so."

"Sorry, I...um...could I check you into a hotel?"

"No, thank you. I'll be just fine. I'll move the couch in front of the door or something."

He tapped his chest. "I'll sleep on the couch."

Her head jerked up. "Not necessary, I'll—"

Melanie figured his uncertainty was a sign
of guilt. "Why did you go behind my back? You didn't
have to ride in on your white horse and rescue me. I
don't need your help."

"I know." He tightened his jaw.

"So why?" Tears burned behind her eyes, but she
would sooner marry Graham Stewart than let Seth see
them. She held his gaze, using every bit of her energy to
keep her tear ducts from overflowing. Her breath rasped
in short bursts, and she fought to control that as well.

Seth squinted and scratched Daisy behind her ears.
"Have you ever seen Atlantic puffins?"

"I don't...what?" His question was so unexpected
Melanie could only stare.

"Puffins. Water birds. They have colorful beaks and
come ashore to lay their eggs. This time of year—"

"I know what puffins are." She spoke more sharply
than she meant to.

"Have you ever seen them?"

"No. But I don't—"

"Daisy and I were just headed out in the boat. Come
with us."

Melanie would have stomped her foot if it wouldn't
have ruined every bit of her credibility. "Seth, I don't
want to see any birds. I came here for an explanation."

"And I'll give you one. But I want you to see the
puffins." He turned and walked into the house, leaving
the door open.

"I insist. Just because this is a sleepy town doesn't mean you can leave your front door wide open."

"I really don't feel comfortable with that arrangement."

Seth turned fully toward her. "It's either the couch, or I'm camping on your porch."

She pushed her lips together, blinking.

He thought she looked like she was thinking of an argument. "Lock your bedroom door."

"A lot of good it did me last time." She raised her brows as she glanced toward the broken front door.

Seth smiled. She wasn't completely comfortable, but at least, she wasn't arguing.

Melanie disappeared into her bedroom and returned with a pillow and blanket, setting them on the couch. She didn't look directly at him. "You know where the bathroom is. And there's cereal and milk if you get hungry. And bananas."

"Thanks," Seth said, thinking her attempt to act as hostess in the bizarre situation was adorable.

"Good night." Melanie shut the door and clicked the lock.

"Night." Seth pushed a kitchen chair against the front door to hold it closed. He turned off the light and laid on the couch, tacoing the pillow behind his head and inhaling the smell of Melanie Owen. Feeling something lumpy beneath his back, he twisted and pulled out the teddy bear. Even the damn Yankees couldn't snuff out the glow left behind by Melanie's voice.

****

Melanie woke to the sound of digital birds chirping. She felt around the nightstand for the disposable phone, turned off the alarm, and sank back into her pillow, wondering why she felt so tired. The events of the night before came back in a rush, bringing a slew of emotions—from fear to embarrassment to something that she couldn't describe, but it made her stomach flutter. She sat up, scooting back against the headboard and hugging her knees. Her gaze moved to her bedroom door.

Seth Goodwyn is asleep on my couch.

She remembered his face when he crashed into her apartment. His eyes were intense and...worried? The stomach flutter came again. And this time, she fought against it. Dr. Goodwyn was the last person she wanted to be involved with. Sure, he was handsome possessing purposely mussed blond hair with bleached tips, sky blue eyes, tanned skin, and broad shoulders. And that smile...Looks-wise, he was perfect. But Seth was absolutely wrong for her.

He was a take-charge kind of guy, strong, a protector. Someone who would tell her what to do—or even do it for her. That type, she avoided like the plague. Some girls liked being taken care of, but Melanie had been running from men like him her entire life.

She'd agonized long and hard over what about her drew the "hero" type. And concluded her shyness and slight stature were like a beacon to men certain she needed to be watched over. Her habit of listening and observing, instead of talking, must seem like uncertainty. Then before she knew it, someone else was in control. Thinking they were babying her, the men took charge and took over.

Melanie was tired of being dominated. She was twenty-five years old, and in her entire life, she had hardly made a decision for herself. Until a month ago when she finally got up the nerve, and she left.

But running away was for kids. So, why couldn't she just move to a town and get a regular job without having to sneak away in the middle of the night, leaving her credit cards and social security number behind, lie about her name, and find a job that paid her "under the table?" She knew exactly why: image. The only thing that mattered to her parents.

Her entire life had been about keeping up appearances. Wearing the right clothes, having the right friends, attending the best prep school and university. Maintaining the persona chosen for her. Smiling for the cameras, acting like the all-around perfect daughter.

The one time she'd done something without asking for permission—joining the girls' softball team at her prep school—had sent her father through the roof. Not being one for confrontation, Melanie had gone along with his wishes and quit. She'd never owned a pet, gone camping, or been to a high school dance. Everything in her life had followed someone else's agenda, and with another campaign season on the horizon, Melanie'd had enough.

She tiptoed to the door, pressed her ear against it, but she couldn't hear anything. Was Seth still asleep? Had he left? Slowly, she turned the knob, startling at the click when it unlocked, and peeked out. The sun rose early in the summer in Maine. In the soft light filtering through her airy curtains, she could see a pair of stockinged feet on the arm of the couch.

She pulled open the door wider and took a cautious step, and then another, praying the floor wouldn't creak.

The feet didn't move. She peeked over the back of

the couch and couldn't contain her grin.

Seth slept with one arm flung over his face, and the other holding her bear to his chest. His mouth was open, and he breathed deeply but didn't snore.

She pulled her gaze away before he woke up and saw her watching. And her glance landed on two magazines on the floor. They must have gotten pushed off the coffee table in the confusion of the night before. The sight of her father's face on the cover of *Politicians Weekly* jolted her. She crept around the couch and lifted the magazine, not wanting Seth to browse through it and see a picture of the senator's family. She hurried back to her room, crammed the magazine into the trash can, grabbed a change of clothes, and darted into the bathroom.

The last time she'd seen her father he'd been the polar opposite of the smiling, handsome senator on the magazine cover.

A month earlier after Sunday dinner, Chuck, her dad's campaign manager, had come over to discuss the game plan for the upcoming election. He'd been worried Senator Rutherford's rating had slipped in the polls. He thought a special interest story about the senator's personal life that voters could relate with would give just the boost he needed.

Chuck had recommended that Melanie should have a boyfriend. The paparazzi would, of course, take shots of the couple dating and sharing intimate moments. They would arrange an engagement in a beautiful setting just before the primaries. Then to cap it all off, an interview with the senator where he became choked up talking about seeing his baby girl as a bride would appeal to every constituent.

Chuck even had the perfect guy picked out—Graham Stewart, heir to his father's pharmaceutical company and manager of a children's charitable organization.

Melanie had met Graham once or twice, and from their few conversations, she was sure he had aspirations to a political office himself.

She listened to Chuck's plan, maintaining a pleasant face and nodding as she knew she was supposed to. But inside, her stomach burned like acid. Once Chuck had left, she confronted her parents in her father's study, hands on hips, leaning forward. "You honestly want me to get engaged to Graham Stewart? To pretend I'm in love with him so you can win another election?"

Her father remained in his seat behind his desk and motioned with a jerk of his head to his wife. A feminine outburst was a job for her to handle.

Donna crossed the room, smoothing back her thick blonde hair, and put an arm around Melanie's shoulders. "You won't need to pretend. He comes from such a respectable family, and don't you think he's handsome?"

Melanie's head felt light. "Mom, I don't even like Graham. And this expectation is too much. I can't fake an engagement."

Her mother turned to face her, brushing the hair off Melanie's forehead. She furrowed her brow as she shook her head. "Oh, Melanie. Honey."

The sympathetic look didn't fool Melanie at all. Her mother had never been one for tenderness. And she didn't pull off the motherly concern tone at all.

"You are old enough to start thinking about these things. We don't want people to wonder why the senator's daughter is still single. They might think there's something…unusual…about you." She frowned, her lip pouting. "And we can't have that."

Her words made Melanie's shoulders clench like someone had taken a rake to a chalkboard. "Isn't it enough that I've done this my entire life? Every single outfit I've worn, party I've gone to, friend I've had, has been chosen for me—for him." She pointed to her father.

He rose and leaned his palms on the desk, narrowing his eyes in a look of warning.

But now that she'd started, Melanie couldn't stop. "This is going too far. You'd really give away my future, sell me to a man, just to win a few votes?"

Her mother gasped.

"How dare you?" Her father's voice boomed through the room. "You selfish girl. This is for our family—for all of us."

Melanie flinched. She lowered her head. Every instinct in her body screamed at her to apologize and hide. But she had to do this now, or never. She held up her head. "No, Dad. This is for you. Everything's always been for you."

Her mind was so lost in the memory that she didn't realize she was crying until a sob choked out of her throat. She clapped a hand over her mouth, hoping Seth hadn't heard it. Leaning her head back, she let the stream of water wash off her tears while she rinsed out the shampoo.

The memory of how her father had grabbed her arm and shaken her while he yelled until he was red in the face made her sob again. She remembered every horrible thing he'd said. The insults, the curses. And her mother had just watched. Let him hurt and berate her only daughter.

Melanie had realized if she stayed in this life, she was on course to end up just like her mother. Nodding, smiling for the camera, never having an opinion, and doing whatever she was told.

So Melanie left.

Finding her way alone was so much harder than she'd thought. She had to keep reminding herself that she was doing the right thing, but the truth was, she missed her home and her nice things, she even missed her mother—but not her father. Just seeing his face on the television, and the magazine cover made her stomach clench.

She knew he was searching for her. Even though he didn't make the search public. Of course he wouldn't. He wouldn't ever reveal anything that might hurt his reputation. For all he knew, Melanie was lying in a morgue somewhere, but he wouldn't let word get out that she was gone. That didn't work out for his happy family man scenario.

Getting out was the first major decision she'd ever made. And she was never going back. Never.

And now, of course she was attracted to the same kind of person. Cocky, rich. She could tell Seth Goodwyn came from money. His gold watch that was probably a graduation present, the expensive polo shirt and deck shoes he wore so casually. As a doctor, he held an influential position in the town, and she wanted nothing to do with a high-profile, powerful person. In her experience, money didn't equal freedom. Exactly the opposite. And she was done being controlled.

Besides he was a Red Sox fan. And that was just

gross.

Once she'd regained control of her emotions, she turned off the water and stepped out of the shower. She blow-dried her hair, got dressed, and put on some mascara before opening the bathroom door.

Seth waved from the kitchen table. "Mornin', sunshine!" He'd poured himself a bowl of cereal and set out another bowl for Melanie.

The flash of his smile sent a ripple through her stomach. "Good morning." She turned away so he couldn't see her reaction, throwing her night clothes into her bedroom. Her blush had subsided by the time she joined him, tying on her blue barista apron. "How did you sleep?"

"Great, considering my sleeping companion." He pointed toward the Jeter bear sitting on the arm of the couch.

Melanie didn't tell him that it looked as though he and furry Jeter had gotten along perfectly well. She wouldn't let it slip that she'd peeked at him while he was sleeping. The thought threatened to bring back the blush. "I'm glad."

"Can I make you breakfast?" He motioned with his spoon to the cereal box.

"No, thank you. I'll get something at work." She rubbed her arms and remained standing. Somehow sitting down to breakfast with him felt too intimate.

"I'll make some calls and get your door fixed. Okay if I hang around here today?"

"You don't have to do that."

"I don't mind. It's my day off. I'll grab my computer from my car and catch up on some stuff. You have a Wi-Fi password?"

"No, sorry."

He glanced at the doorframe and squinted. "How about a tape measure?"

She shook her head.

"I bet I can get one downstairs."

"Thanks." Melanie looked at the clock on the wall. "I need to go." She grabbed her purse, and the discomfort of the situation—Seth eating breakfast in her kitchen, sending her off to work, and acting so at ease with the entire thing—made looking him in the eyes impossible.

"I'll see ya later?"

"I'll bring over your Caffe Americano on my break." She spoke over her shoulder as she pulled away the chair blocking the door and hurried outside.

Melanie's heart was rushing as she crossed the street and cut through the corner of the park by the community center. She needed to get ahold of herself and remember that Seth Goodwyn was completely wrong for her. The resolution was difficult to remember when his smile kept floating to the surface of her thoughts.

Chapter Two

Seth watched the door swing behind Melanie. He rinsed off the cereal bowl, put the milk into the fridge, and made a call to the hardware store, looking for a handyman to repair the doorframe. After a few more phone calls, he had an appointment to meet "Willie" in an hour.

He folded the blanket he'd used and straightened the pillows on the couch, rolling his eyes when he looked at Melanie's teddy bear. *Jeter, really?*

He thought about Melanie's quick departure and wondered what had changed. Last night, he felt like he'd broken through her defenses and seen just a flash of the real Melanie. But this morning, her wall was back in place, and he didn't understand why.

Maybe he could attribute it to catching her by surprise, but her reserve had felt like more than that. They'd connected—even if it was briefly. For a few moments, she laughed and joked, and he saw a completely different side. How could he get back there? How could he find the real Melanie again?

Walking around her apartment, he realized that, other than the Yankee teddy bear, nothing personal was here. No pictures, no books, no calendar on the wall. Not even a computer. He remembered seeing a few magazines the night before, and he found a monthly sports periodical in a jumble under the coffee table. He smoothed it out and smiled at the cover—of course, it was a special Derek Jeter issue.

Baseball—even if it was Yankee baseball—was one thing he knew Melanie loved. He glanced under the coffee table for the other magazine, certain there had been two. He looked behind the couch and wondered if Melanie had moved it during the night. Had she come out of her room while he was asleep? The thought sent heat over his skin. He didn't hate the idea.

Glancing once more around the space, he stepped toward Melanie's bedroom door. Now that he wasn't chasing an imaginary attacker, looking in her room felt like an invasion of privacy. But she *had* left him in her apartment alone, hadn't she?

From the doorway, he glanced around the room, seeing nothing but her bed, a dresser, and the closet he'd thrown open the night before. The starkness of her private space reinforced what he'd already concluded. Melanie was hiding. She'd run away from a dangerous situation, taking nothing but her clothing. He brushed aside the hanging clothes, noting the name brands. Her clothes were expensive. What kind of life had she left behind? And why?

The surge of protectiveness he always felt when he thought about Melanie being afraid or hurt returned with a strength that surprised him. She needed him, and if he could learn how to help her, he needed to find out what she was hiding from.

He turned, and something caught his eye, the magazine he'd seen the night before was in the trashcan next to the door. Fishing it out, he studied the cover. Senator Rutherford of Illinois. Was *Melanie interested in politics, as well as baseball*?

Leaning against the doorframe, he thumbed through the issue, studying pictures of Senator Rutherford during his various campaigns and terms in Washington. He turned a page and froze. The picture's caption indicated the senator's family was vacationing at a ski cabin in Colorado. He leaned against a wooden railing with his wife and daughter. Even though most of her hair was covered by a ski cap, and she was a few years younger, Seth had no doubt. Melanie Owen was really Melanie Rutherford.

Melanie's father was one of the most powerful men in America.

He searched the article carefully, piecing together what he could about Melanie. She'd attended private schools and an Ivy League University, worked as a docent at the Art Institute of Chicago, and served on the boards of various charities.

No mention was made of a boyfriend or a husband. Why had this woman left her privileged life to live in a run-down apartment and work as a barista in a small New England fishing town?

He returned the magazine to the trash and sat on the couch, turning over the bear in his hands without really noticing.

Seth's entire view of Melanie flipped completely around. She wasn't a woman without resources or education, but she'd been raised in elite circles. She'd attended the very finest schools the country had to offer, and she had the ability to go anywhere or do anything she wanted. So, what had happened to make her run from all of this?

A knock sounded, shaking Seth out of his contemplations.

"Looks like ya got a busted door." A short man with thick dark hair and a tool belt stood in the doorway.

"You must be Willie." Seth crossed the room and shook his hand. "Thanks for coming."

Willie bent down and peered at the splintered wood. He pulled a tape measure from his tool belt and stretched it from the floor to the top of the doorway, muttering to himself. "Door's standard size. Job won't take more than a few hours."

"No problem. Will you be able to get it done today?"

"Yah, sure, sure." Willie wrote something down on a notepad. "Just gotta make a run to the lumber yard, and I'll get started."

Sitting back on the couch, Seth tried to make sense of what he'd discovered. Why would Melanie keep her identity a secret? What had happened to her?

He thought through what he knew about the woman. Not much, he realized as he glanced around the apartment once more on his way outside.

Stopping at Murphy's Bar, he got the Wi-Fi password from David Hu, and then crossed the street to the clinic's parking lot for his computer bag.

Once he was back at Melanie's kitchen table, he opened his laptop and started his investigation. Entering the name Melanie Rutherford brought up articles about the senator. He scanned through for information about his daughter, but he didn't find much more than he'd read in the magazine article.

Clicking on the "images" tab, he found picture after picture of Melanie, college graduation, family vacations, giving a speech, attending a charity function with her parents.

The Melanie in the pictures surprised him. She appeared poised, collected, immaculately dressed, with not a hair out of place. Having met her and knowing she tended to be less showy and more reserved, he wondered if the photos had been posed.

Though he did not know Melanie well, the fact that no baseball paraphernalia appeared in any pictures stuck out like a neon sign. The only thing he'd known her to feel any excitement about was conspicuously missing from over a hundred images.

The door creaked open.

Seth shut his laptop and stood when he saw Melanie enter. He took the offered cup from her, hoping his expression looked innocent. "Thanks. I didn't know Sang Freud's delivers."

She handed him a box. "It's a blueberry scone. Not your usual, but I thought you might like it."

He lifted the cardboard lid, peeking inside. "Smells terrific." He took a bite. "Mmmm. You must be psychic." He wiped crumbs from the corner of his mouth." This is seriously the best scone I've ever had. I should have been asking you all along for recommendations, instead of sticking with the chocolate chip muffins."

Seeing Melanie's soft smile, Seth thought how nice that she didn't just spout empty words. She spoke if there was something to say, but didn't chatter to fill the silence. "Willie the handyman is on his way with supplies. He thinks your door will be repaired in just a few hours."

She ran her finger over the Formica of the kitchen table. "Thanks for taking care of that." She glanced up and lowered her eyes. "And for sticking around. I should have told you earlier."

"Anytime." Seth studied her. Melanie's posture was straight, she spoke clearly, but her voice was soft. Knowing more about her history, he saw her in a new light. Unlike his first impression, he didn't think she appeared to be afraid so much as shy. Melanie had a quiet confidence that he thought many would mistake for insecurity. He certainly had.

"I really could have done all this." She waved her hand toward the doorframe.

"I know."

Briefly, she met his gaze with wide eyes.

Seth thought her expression looked surprised at his reply. "How about if *you* break something at *my* house, it's your turn to call Willie."

"Deal." Melanie's smile grew.

The twist of a smirk returned to her lips, making Seth's heart flip.

"I better get back to work. Thanks again."

After he saw the door close behind her, Seth opened his computer and studied the photos again. The more time he spent with Melanie, the less he could see of her true self in the pictures. The light in her smile was absent.

He read through the captions beneath the pictures. *Melanie, daughter of Senator Rutherford, speaks to constituents at charity event. Daughter of Senator Rutherford graduated magna cum laude. Senator Rutherford's daughter follows in her father's footsteps, giving back to the community.*

Seth pushed his hands through his hair, blowing out a sigh as he realized not one sentence was about Melanie as a person. She was portrayed solely as her father's daughter. Is that why the light was missing from her eyes? Was she unhappy?

He shook his head, telling himself to calm down. *Stop jumping to conclusions when you have no facts.* But something told him he was right.

Now that he knew more about her, he didn't see her as a victim but as a woman who was shy and lost in her world. Whatever she was figuring out, she must need to do it here in Lobster Cove as Melanie Owen. And Seth wouldn't take away that freedom.

Willie returned with the cut pieces of wood, and Seth helped him tear out the broken frame and replace it, then apply a few coats of paint. The handyman had been right—the doorframe was as good as new in a few hours.

After saying goodbye to Willie, Seth found a broom and cleaned up the wood shavings. Then, since he had no other reason to stay at her apartment, he took the keys from the hook by the front door to drop off at the coffee house and left, checking the lock behind him. As he walked down the metal staircase, he saw Benny from the city offices had taken a few steps up the stairs.

When he saw Seth coming down, he returned to the bottom and waited. "Is Miss Owen at home?"

"No, she's working. I'm headed over there now if you want me to give her a message." Seth felt a twist of guilt, knowing that he should stay out of Melanie's private business, but the need to watch over her won out.

"Ya, let her know that the co-ed softball team she wanted to start up can't happen. City Council thinks it's a great idea, but the recreation department just doesn't have that kind of funding."

Melanie had looked into starting a softball team?

That didn't sound like someone who wasn't planning to remain in town. And thinking of her wearing a ball cap and coaching a group of kids warmed his midsection. She'd be great at it. Maybe this is just what she needed to feel like she could do things on her own. Seth scratched his cheek. "What about a sponsor?"

"Yeah, suppose that would work." Benny squinted and nodded. "Don't know who, maybe a parent of a kid on the team?"

Melanie wouldn't thank him for interfering, but he wanted this for her. He wanted her to be happy, to have the light in her eyes and the sassy grin. "How about an anonymous sponsor?"

****

"Keep running!" Melanie yelled. "All the way home!" She clapped as Joe rounded the last base and windmilled her arms to bring him in to home plate.

He slid into the base, and the team cheered.

Melanie looked around the ball diamond and couldn't hold back a smile. She couldn't believe the city had approved her request to coach a team, but she was thrilled when Seth came into the coffee shop a few weeks earlier with the news. A few flyers placed in shop windows around town, and before she knew it, fifteen boys and girls were registered.

Most of the kids that showed up today to their first practice had no idea how to play ball, but they caught on quickly. She was already thinking through the batting order and seeing which kids would be best in which positions. This team would take a lot of work, but the excitement of doing something she loved, and helping others to love it too grew in her chest like a balloon. And best of all, her father wasn't here to disapprove.

From the corner of her eye, she recognized a car pull into the park by the baseball diamonds. When she saw Benny driving, she waved.

Benny climbed out, carrying a large box. Melanie had met him at the city offices once or twice and thought he was probably a few years younger than she was. His hair was dark and a little greasy, but he was friendly in a nervous sort of way. She was glad he was the one in charge of the rec department.

Melanie blew her whistle, waving her hand to gather the players in the infield. "Okay, team, everyone get a drink, and I think our uniforms are here."

With Benny's help, she handed out jerseys and ball caps, pulling down her own cap on her head. Once hats had been adjusted and each player had a shirt that fit, Melanie stepped back and admired the team in their red jerseys. The Lobster Cove Trawlers was officially a team, and Melanie had done this herself. She wondered if she'd ever stop smiling.

She spoke for a moment to the parents, passing out practice and game schedules then helped Benny clean up the bags and wrappers from the uniforms. Two hats remained in the bottom of the box. "Benny, you don't have a hat." She held one toward him.

He crammed on the hat. "Thanks. Maybe you should give the other to Dr. Goodwyn."

At the mention of Seth's name, Melanie blinked and her heart skipped. He still came into the coffee house every morning, and whether she wanted to admit it or not, his arrival had become the thing she looked forward to most. She'd even worked out with Carlos to take her break earlier and joined Seth a few times as he drank his coffee.

Had Benny seen them chatting in the coffee house window? Did he assume she and Seth were in a relationship? Her cheeks heated and she tried to keep her feelings from showing on her face. She glanced at the hat in her hand. "Dr. Goodwyn? Why would he want a hat?"

"Sometimes sponsors—" Benny sucked in and made his mouth into an "o." His face turned red.

"What do you mean, *sponsors*?" Melanie's light heart grew heavy.

Benny shrugged. "I was thinking about something else. Um, can you grab those bags?" He lifted the box and started toward his car.

She put her hand on the box. "Wait. Are you saying Dr. Goodwyn sponsored the Trawlers?"

His gaze darted around, not looking directly at her. "Listen, I wasn't supposed to say anything. He wanted to keep it anonymous."

Melanie's stomach shrank. All the excitement of her team, the pride she'd taken in doing this herself—It wasn't hers at all. Why had Seth done this? The familiar heaviness settled onto her shoulders. Seth was working behind the scenes, pulling strings that she didn't even know about. He was taking control of her life.

The sick feeling grew into a burn, fueled by anger. Why did men think she was incapable of doing things herself? Why did they need to have power over her? She should have trusted her initial instinct about Seth. He was no different than her father.

Benny grimaced. "Yeah, I really wasn't supposed to say anything…"

Melanie could only nod as she decided what to do about his disclosure. Melanie Rutherford would smile shyly and keep her real feelings to herself. But what would Melanie Owen do? She followed Benny back to the parking lot, her mind in a whirl.

"Need a ride back to town?"

"I've got my bike." She pointed to where her bicycle leaned against the bleachers.

Benny put the box in his car. "Hey, listen. I'm really sorry I let that sponsor thing slip. Seems like it upset ya."

"Oh no. Not at all." She willed a smile to her face and shrugged. "Maybe I will take the hat to Dr. Goodwyn. You don't happen to know where he lives, do you?"

****

After dropping off the baseball equipment at her apartment, Melanie rode through the outskirts of Lobster Cove, admiring the grand old houses on quiet, tree-lined streets. The road left behind the residential areas and followed the shoreline along a cliff. As she rode uphill, her thighs burned, but her fury burned hotter. She didn't even know if Seth would be home. But at the moment, she didn't care. She'd camp out on his front porch if she had to.

According to Benny, Seth had bought a vacation cottage in a hidden cove. She imagined his "bachelor pad"—expensive contemporary furnishings, gourmet kitchen, and high-end art and electronics. And he probably had a sleek sail boat. The very type of person she'd left her old life behind to escape. Why had she let down her guard?

Beneath the road, various boats bobbed, small islands rose here and there in the ocean, and she heard the far-off blast of a fog horn. She glanced down at the ball cap hanging on her handlebars. If she hadn't been so angry, she might have stopped to admire the view.

Following Benny's directions, she turned onto a road that led through the trees. The forest muffled the crunch of her tires, and she strained harder to push her pedals on the gravel. Finally, she came to an old wooden fence and the turn-off Benny described. She stopped, setting down her feet and breathing heavily. Peering down the road, she couldn't see any house between the thick trees.

Turning onto the side road and winding downhill through the shade was a relief. The steepness of the incline made her clench her brakes. And just as Benny had said, the road opened and she was suddenly at sea level. A yellow country house with red shutters and white trim stood alone in the cove. The house was beautiful. And the setting, beyond anything she could have imagined. She glanced back, but the road behind her disappeared into the trees. The spot was secluded with cliffs and forest surrounding. Melanie stopped, completely enchanted by the scene.

From around the corner of the house, a large golden retriever bounded toward her, barking.

Melanie put a foot back onto her pedal, ready to ride away if the dog was threatening. "Good dog," she said. That Seth might have a pet hadn't occurred to her. "Sit."

The dog sat, its tongue lolling out of its mouth and its tail thumping against the ground.

Melanie relaxed and swung her leg over the bike. "Good, okay then." Accompanied by her new friend, she walked her bike up the gravel drive and leaned it against the porch rail then climbed up the wooden steps. On a brass plaque next to the front door were the words, "Hyne House." She wondered about the words, but not enough to ask. This wasn't a social visit.

Melanie squared her shoulders, straightened her T-shirt and, taking a calming breath, rang the bell.

After a moment, Seth opened the door, wearing worn khaki shorts, a blue button-down rolled to his elbows, and a puzzled expression that softened into a smile "Mel."

She pushed away the breathless feeling his appearance and the warm way he said her name created. He was the only person who'd ever called her Mel, and she hated that she loved it.

He glanced down. "I see you met Daisy."

At the sound of her name, the dog walked to him and pushed her head under his hand.

"Come on in. How was practice?"

Melanie held out the hat. "They sent an extra hat for the sponsor."

His brow furrowed, and the skin around his eyes tightened. He took the ball cap and lifted his gaze to the matching hat she wore. "Thanks." He spoke the word slowly.

Melanie figured his uncertainty was a sign of guilt. "Why did you go behind my back? You didn't have to ride in on your white horse and rescue me. I don't need your help."

"I know." He tightened his jaw.

"So why?" Tears burned behind her eyes, but she would sooner marry Graham Stewart than let Seth see them. She held his gaze, using every bit of her energy to keep her tear ducts from overflowing. Her breath rasped in short bursts, and she fought to control that as well.

Seth squinted and scratched Daisy behind her ears. "Have you ever seen Atlantic puffins?"

"I don't…what?" His question was so unexpected Melanie could only stare.

"Puffins. Water birds. They have colorful beaks and come ashore to lay their eggs. This time of year—"

"I know what puffins are." She spoke more sharply than she meant to.

"Have you ever seen them?"

"No. But I don't—"

"Daisy and I were just headed out in the boat. Come with us."

Melanie would have stomped her foot if it wouldn't have ruined every bit of her credibility. "Seth, I don't want to see any birds. I came here for an explanation."

"And I'll give you one. But I want you to see the puffins." He turned and walked into the house, leaving the door open.

Daisy glanced back at Melanie then followed her master.

His response had completely thrown Melanie off. She'd expected a denial or a half-explanation, something condescending that implied she didn't understand. Or even anger at Benny for telling her the truth. But she hadn't expected Seth to be open and cheerful. Out of curiosity, she stepped inside.

Seth's house was nothing like she'd imagined: hardwood floors, cozy-looking country furniture, and a large stone fireplace made up the living room. She followed his voice past the stairs to the kitchen and felt immediately warm and comfortable. White cabinets lined the room, and a round wooden table sat in an alcove surrounded by windows. The view of the bay was breathtaking.

"Thought I'd make us a picnic." Seth spoke from behind the refrigerator door. He stepped out and set an armful of food on the counter.

Daisy sat to the side of the island, watching every move he made.

"Can I help?" Melanie asked.

"Sure." He set a loaf of bread on the counter. "Why don't you wash off the grapes?" Seth opened a cupboard and pulled out a colander, setting it next to the sink.

Melanie rounded the counter and poured in the grapes, rinsing them off.

Seth offered a plastic bowl with a lid, and then set a worn-out cooler on the counter. "Sorry, no picnic basket. Daisy and I make do with this old thing."

While Melanie filled the bowl with grapes, she watched Seth out of the corner of her eye as he worked in the kitchen. He moved naturally around the space, and she found it fascinating to watch. She'd never seen a man so comfortable in a kitchen.

Once the picnic was loaded, Seth wiped off the counter with a rag. "Hang on a sec." He left the room and returned with a plaid blanket and some sweatshirts. Handing them to Melanie, he slung on his backpack, lifted the cooler, and then jerked his head toward a back door.

Melanie opened it then followed him and Daisy outside. They walked across the wide porch, down the wooden stairs, over a rocky beach to a narrow dock that led about twenty yards out into the cove.

A boat bobbed at the end of the wooden walkway.

Seth pulled on the rope to bring the boat next to the dock. He hopped inside, and the dog leapt in after him.

"All aboard." He took the bundle from her and offered his hand.

Melanie looked from the craft to Seth. It was hardly more than a rowboat with a motor. She placed her hand in his, and heat from his touch flowed over her skin. As she glanced up, her gaze met Seth's, and she realized how close they were.

His mouth spread into a slow grin, white against his tan.

Melanie's heart tumbled like it was doing somersaults. She released his hand and sat hard, holding onto the metal bench as the boat teetered. Bending her head forward, she took off the ball cap to let her hair fall and cover her face. *Just calm down.* She breathed slowly, running her fingers over Daisy's golden fur and waiting for her flush to fade.

Seth opened a trunk and handed her a life vest, then put on his own. "I should have asked if you get sea sick."

Melanie shook her head and slipped her arms into the vest, buckling it over her chest. She dared a glance and felt heat flood her cheeks at the sight of his grin. She turned, her nerves tingling and wondered how she could feel so comfortable with someone and so nervous at the same time.

Chapter Three

Seth unhooked the rope from the dock and started the motor. The propeller kept perfect time with his chaotic heartbeat. To say he'd been surprised when he'd opened the door and seen Melanie on his doorstep was an understatement. She'd looked ready to burst from anger, and a sick coil twisted his stomach when he'd realized Benny told her Seth had sponsored the team. But, he figured she would have found out about it sooner or later. Secrets didn't last long in a town of this size.

He steered the boat out of the bay, carefully making his way between clusters of black rocks jutting out of the water, and continued up the coast. The view of the cliffs above with their crest of pine trees never failed to amaze him. But even more awe-inspiring was the sight of the woman riding with him. From his seat in the stern, he saw her lift her gaze to the tops of the cliffs. Her light hair flew behind, looking like a silk curtain. As soon as the thought entered his mind he rolled his eyes. *A silk curtain? Really?* The effect Melanie had on him was ridiculous.

Daisy rested her head on Melanie's leg.

Seth watched for a reaction, but Melanie just laid a hand on the dog's head. And the sight warmed his heart. He couldn't believe she'd agreed to join them. But then again, he hadn't left her much choice in the matter.

Melanie wanted an explanation, and he would have to give it. But for now, he'd just enjoy the sight of her and worry later about what to say.

The boat rounded a bend and over the sound of the motor, he saw, rather than heard, Melanie gasp.

The cliffs were covered with white puffins—some roosting, some diving and flying. Colorful parents tended to their small gray, fluffy babies. Birds walked along the rocks and bobbed in the water.

She looked back, catching his gaze and pointed ahead.

Seth nodded and gave a thumbs-up. He cut the motor and guided the boat to a clump of rocks. The small island was close enough to afford a good view of the puffins, but far enough away not to disturb them. He jumped out and pulled the boat as close as he could, securing it with the rope.

The water came half way up his calves, but it wasn't deep enough to get Melanie's shorts wet. He was glad. Sitting in cold clothes would make for a miserable evening once the sun got low. "You might want to take off your shoes." He held onto the side of the boat and reached an arm toward her.

She slipped off her tennis shoes and took Seth's hand. She teetered as she stepped over the side of the boat and grabbed onto his shoulder.

He hooked an arm around her waist and eased her into the water. "Careful, the rocks are uneven." He spoke to cover the awkwardness of holding her in his arms.

Melanie nodded and stepped back, not meeting his eye. She pulled the ball cap back onto her head.

Daisy jumped, landing mostly on the rocks and only

splashing them a bit.

They unloaded the boat and found a flat place to spread out the blanket.

Melanie sat next to him, her gaze on the cliffs. She pointed at a puffin running across the water. The bird left a trail of splashes before getting the momentum to take off. Another dove into the water, emerging with a squirming fish in its colorful beak.

Seth pulled a pair of binoculars from his backpack and offered them to Melanie.

She trained them on the birds across the water.

And he found it every bit as charming to study her smile beneath the lenses as she watched. "What do ya think?" Seth asked.

She lowered the binoculars and exchanged them for a sandwich. "They're adorable. Their round cheeks and sad eyes. They look like clowns, don't they? Especially their bright orange feet."

The explosion of words was more than Seth thought he'd ever heard from her at one time. He looked through the binoculars. "I know, there's something so comical about the way they walk."

They sat quietly for a moment, Seth pretending to watch the birds while every sense was tuned in to the woman sitting beside him.

"Can Daisy have some of my sandwich? She's looking a little hungry."

He pulled down the binoculars. "Is she bugging you? I can tell her to get lost."

"No. I just don't know what dogs can eat."

"Haven't you ever had a dog?"

Melanie shook her head.

"Just don't give her any chocolate. And I try not to

let her have fruit. Sensitive stomach, you know."

She broke off a bit of her sandwich and offered it to Daisy, jerking away her hand when the dog took it.

"She won't bite you."

"Good girl, Daisy." Melanie spoke in a soft voice. She gave the dog another bite of sandwich and patted her head. Once the food was gone, she brushed off her legs. "Thanks for bringing me here, Seth."

The sound of her saying his name made his heart squeeze. "I love this place."

"Let me guess, your dad used to bring you out to watch the puffins when you were a kid."

He shook his head. "My dad wasn't really the outdoorsy type."

Melanie shrugged. "Mine either." She kept her gaze on the puffins.

Seth tried to imagine the tuxedo-wearing Senator Rutherford he'd seen on TV riding in a rusty boat and sitting on a scratchy blanket with the wind blowing his perfectly styled silver hair, and he found he couldn't do it. He saw Melanie's brows pull together and bumped her arm. "Thinking about your family?"

"A little."

"Where are ya from, Mel?"

"Here and there." When the wind picked up, she held onto the brim of her cap. "I mostly grew up in DC. At least that's where I went to high school. What about you? No wait, let me see. You don't talk like you're from Maine, and you're a Sox fan. My guess is Boston."

"You got that right." Seth grinned and noticed she didn't turn away.

"So, why Lobster Cove?"

"I could ask you the same question."

Melanie pulled her knees to her chest, patting Daisy's head when the dog made a protesting whine at the loss of her headrest. "You go first."

"After med school, I just couldn't figure out where to settle down, ya know? My dad had a position for me at a hospital in Boston, but after a few months, I…I guess it just didn't fit. I didn't want to just be known as Leonard Goodwyn's son. After spending my entire life trying to be perfect for my parents, I wanted to find my own way."

Melanie tipped her head to the side, leaning her cheek on her knee.

She watched him with an expression he couldn't quite identify, but she was interested in what he said, so he kept talking. "I came up to Acadia to do some hiking, I guess to find my head and figure out what I wanted. I pulled into this little town and fell in love. The people, the community, the ocean, everything. It just felt like home. It's weird how I didn't feel like that in my actual home, ya know."

"I *do* know."

Seth leaned closer to hear Melanie's quiet voice.

She rested her chin on her knees, staring at the puffin cliff. "I guess we're each looking for something. Funny how we both landed here."

Seth thought if he stayed quiet, she might elaborate. Maybe tell him everything, who she was, why she was hiding. What was she looking for? He hadn't missed how quickly she'd changed the subject when he asked where she was from.

Melanie lifted her head and turned to Seth. "And so what about Daisy? You decided a house isn't a home without a furry friend to share it with?"

The dog raised her head at the sound of her name.

He grinned and snapped his fingers for Daisy to move between them. "Atta, girl," he muttered, scratching the dog's stomach. "I found a half-starved puppy with a broken leg in the forest. Took her to the vet, brought her home, and she stuck around."

"She's lucky you found her."

Seth shrugged. "I sorta feel like the lucky one."

"And why did you name her Daisy?"

He was quiet for a moment before answering. "My sister loved daisies."

Melanie smiled softly and buried her hand in the dog's fur, scratching the other side of Daisy's belly.

The dog's tongue lolled out, and her eyes closed. With both of them scratching her belly, she must think she was in doggie heaven.

Telling about Daisy was the perfect segue way. "Listen, Mel, about the team, I'm sorry. I really shouldn't have butted into something that was none of my business." He pushed his fingers through his hair, praying she'd understand what he was saying. "But when I learned from Benny that the town didn't have the funding. I thought of how disappointed you'd be, and I just couldn't let it happen. Not knowing how much you love baseball."

She rubbed her arm. "I *can* do things myself, you know. I don't need to be rescued all the time."

She'd spoken quickly, almost as if she hadn't thought through her words. Seth felt like she'd pulled back a curtain and let him see backstage—just a glimpse, but it revealed so much. Melanie needed independence, and he was willing to bet she didn't get it at home.

The best way to earn her trust was to reciprocate—pull aside his own curtain and let her see his own secret. "I lost someone—my sister—a long time ago, and I guess trying to save everyone else is my way of making up for it."

"I'm sorry. Do you want...do you want to talk about it?" She stopped scratching Daisy and gave him her attention.

"It's not a very happy story."

"Only if you want to tell me."

Seth shifted, bending his knee and turning toward her. He blew out a breath, hoping to ease the ache in his chest as he remembered the day. "I'd taken Cassie to the park down the street from home. We'd been there a hundred times, and it was close enough we could see our front door from the playground. While we played on the swings, a bee stung her." He picked at the blanket stitching, finding it easier to look at his hand than Melanie. "Nobody knew she was allergic. I had no idea what was wrong. I tried to figure out why she couldn't breathe. I figured she'd been playing too hard and needed to rest. I told her to lay in the shade." He cleared his throat, pushing down the lump that rose when he thought about his sister. "By the time I ran for help...Anyway, you can figure out the rest."

"How old were you?"

"Eight. She was five." Though over twenty years had passed, the tug on his heart was still as strong.

"And that's why you tried to be perfect all the time."

Melanie had only known him a few weeks, but her simple assessment showed how deeply she understood him. He hadn't realized his fists were clenched until she placed a hand over his. He swallowed. "I didn't mean to take over, or to imply you couldn't make the team work without my help, really. I know I shouldn't have interfered, and I'm sorry."

Melanie studied his face. She looked down at Daisy. "You help people." She glanced up and smiled. "And dogs. And you shouldn't apologize for that. I'm sorry I overreacted."

She took a breath like she would say more, but then furrowed her brow and blew it out. The open expression on her face became guarded once again, and he knew his chance of learning more about her had passed.

"I...Thank you, Seth. From me and the kids. Maybe you want to come to a game sometime?"

"I promise I'll let you coach." He held out his hand.

Melanie's face flushed red as she took it and shook. "I wouldn't mind your help."

****

The trip home was silent, but not uncomfortably so. Each seemed lost in personal thoughts. As he remembered spilling his guts, Seth gritted his teeth. *I might as well have handed out hankies for the cry fest.* What in the world made him think he should share something so personal with someone he hardly knew? And what was he doing with her? From the first moment he'd met her, something about Melanie had pulled on him like a magnet. But what was the end game? How long was she staying in Lobster Cove? Was she truly hiding from her family out of fear? Or just making a point?

By the time the boat was docked, the night was nearly dark. The two walked slowly up the pier as if they were reluctant for the night to end.

41

Seth pulled on a sweatshirt and offered one to Melanie. "Let me just grab my keys, and I'll drive ya home."

"My bike…"

"We can put it in the trunk."

On the front porch, Melanie pointed to the plaque by the door. "Hyne House? Is that a family name?"

"The realtor told me a lot of the houses were built by Scottish immigrants. Hyne means something like harbor, or safe."

Melanie drew a breath. "That's beautiful." Her voice was little more than a whisper. She walked ahead of him to the car.

You're safe here, Mel. Seth spoke the words in his mind, wishing he knew what Melanie was hiding from, and wishing he were brave enough to say them aloud.

****

Melanie stood at her apartment window, holding aside the sheer curtain as she watched people gathering for the Fourth of July celebration. The carnival was in full swing at the park by Grant's Lake. Even though the park was nearly two blocks away, the traffic around the town center was heavier than Melanie had seen in Lobster Cove, as drivers searched for a parking spot. She smiled as she watched residents greeting each other and families walking together, small children holding their parents' hands and looking both ways before crossing the street.

She caught sight of a Lobster Cove Trawler hat, and her chest warmed. This feeling of community was something she hadn't realized she'd been missing. Now that she'd lived here for nearly a month, she found the acceptance of the townspeople, their friendship, and the sense of "belonging" made her feel a part of something important.

Why hadn't she felt that way before? She'd served on boards for various charities and knew her work had made a difference. But something as simple as volunteer coaching a kids' softball team seemed so much more significant. And she knew the feeling of pride came down to the motives behind her service. The performance wasn't merely for publicity, or for her father's campaign, or because of her last name. She coached the team for the kids.

She sighed, feeling like a fraud. *What am I doing?* Leaving home had seemed like the exact right thing to do. Showing her father she couldn't be manipulated anymore had been crucial, and she didn't regret her action at all. But now the thought of returning, of leaving Lobster Cove, made her chest feel empty. The situation had become more complicated.

The sight of Seth crossing the street sent a quiver through her stomach. *Much more complicated.*

She tied a sweatshirt around her waist and hurried outside, locking the door behind her and smiling as she always did when the knob clicked into place in the brand new doorframe.

Seth waited at the bottom of the steps.

The excited, nervous, quivery feeling returned, but guilt rose bitter in her throat, making her feel nauseated. What would Seth think if she told him the truth?

He wouldn't understand, or would he? How could he when she didn't understand herself? He would almost certainly be angry at being deceived. How would he react? The sick feeling grew.

Lobster Cove had started to feel like home. And

Seth—her feelings for him were so complicated. He embodied everything she wanted to escape. An important person in town, used to telling people what to do, and if she allowed him, he'd take away her independence. But at the same time, with him, Seth's intentions felt different. Seth had been completely honest with her. He believed helping people would ease his guilt over not saving his sister. Nothing underhanded, nothing deceptive. No ulterior motives. And she sensed he'd sponsored the team because he cared.

But she couldn't stay here forever. Couldn't pretend forever. Her past would catch up with her sooner or later, and when it did, Seth would feel betrayed

"Hey, isn't that the coach of the Lobster Cove Trawlers?" Seth grinned when she reached the sidewalk.

Melanie smiled back, but she was unable to shake the gloom that hung over her.

He turned toward the park. "Just wait until you experience a small town Fourth. Nothing else comes close—" He broke off and pulled his brows together. "Hey, you doing okay?"

"Yeah, of course." Melanie tried to make her smile look as though nothing was bothering her.

He took her arm, pulling her into the sunlight. "You sure? You look a bit pale."

"I'm sure, *Doctor* Goodwyn." She forced her smile wider. His concern warmed her, but she didn't want him to worry—or did she? *What is wrong with me? Pull yourself together and stop acting crazy.* Melanie wanted to roll her eyes at the absurd schoolgirl she was turning into around Seth.

His expression didn't relax. "Let's grab something

to eat before we go to the carnival. Just to make sure your blood sugar isn't too low." He glanced up the road. "How about something from Sweet Bea's? She makes the best Irish brown bread on the planet."

"Sure."

They walked a few shops down. As Seth held open the door to Sweet Bea's, the aroma of home-baked goods flowed out on a wave of Irish music. The interior of the café was warm and inviting with wooden tables and yellow curtains.

"Morning, Beatrice," Seth called.

"Doctor Goodwyn! So nice to see you." Beatrice O'Brien smiled from behind the counter. Her red hair flowed over her shoulders, and her green eyes sparkled. "It's been a few weeks."

"I don't know how I've survived for so long without your brown bread. And it's *Seth* when I'm not wearing a white coat."

"Glad you're back, Seth." Beatrice grinned and glanced at Melanie.

Seth stepped aside. "Have you met Melanie Owen?"

Melanie shrank back. Meeting new people was one of her least-favorite activities. She wished she could chat freely like Seth, but bashfulness was something she constantly battled. She forced her gaze to remain steadily on Beatrice. "Nice to meet you." The words came out softly.

Seth touched the small of her back, just casually.

He understood her shyness and the small gesture of support sent a surge of assurance, spreading as heat from his touch. Just knowing he was there made her feel calm and her nervousness dissipated.

"A pleasure." Beatrice reached over the counter and

shook her hand.

Seth looked between the two women. "Melanie works over at Sang Freud."

Beatrice shot a smirk at Melanie. "That explains why the good doctor hasn't been in for his morning coffee in a few weeks."

Shaking his head, Seth raised his hands. "You caught me."

"How do you like Lobster Cove?" Beatrice leaned her forearms against the counter.

"I love it." Melanie was happy to share her feelings about the place that had started to feel like home. "The town's beautiful, and people have been so friendly."

"Where ya from?"

Melanie felt Seth tense, and knew he was worried about her reluctance to talk about herself. "D.C." She smiled at Seth to show him she was ok. "I was looking for something a little slower paced."

"Well, you sure found it, didn't ya?" Beatrice waved her hand toward the large windows in the front of the café. "Doesn't get much slower paced than good ol' Lobster Cove, that's for sure. Now, what can I get for you two?"

The pair placed their order and sat at a round wooden table near the window.

Beatrice delivered their bread and drinks, setting them on the lace tablecloth. And once she was assured that they didn't need anything further, she walked back through the batwing doors into the kitchen.

Melanie studied the family pictures that hung in elegant frames along the café walls. The sight of smiling parents and children should make her homesick for her own family, but it created a different sort of ache. In over a month, nothing had been said in the news about her disappearance. Knowing her father hushed it up to maintain his reputation hurt worse than the cruel words he'd yelled or the painful way he'd jerked her arm.

She turned her gaze to the man across the table. Seth had his own issues with his family. The pain they must have suffered and his guilt had to have been more than a young child could bear. He'd spoken about trying to be perfect. Probably feeling like he could never do enough to make up for something that he'd been too young to prevent, but had shaped every decision from then on. Based on the few things he'd said, she didn't think his family had been much closer than hers.

When she realized she was staring, she looked down at her plate, breaking off a piece of bread and sticking it in her mouth to cover her discomfiture.

"Bread's great, isn't it?" Seth slathered butter over his slice.

Melanie nodded as she chewed.

"And make sure you drink some juice."

She glanced up and raised a brow.

"Sorry, I'm just being a doctor for a little while until I'm sure you're okay."

Melanie had to admit his concern made her feel important. Somehow, the way Seth watched over her didn't leave her with the frustration of feeling dependent or helpless.

When she'd left home, she had vowed never to allow a man to call the shots over her life. Were a pair of blue eyes and a white grin changing her position? She glanced up, studying him as he wiped a napkin over his mouth. Seth didn't seem capable of violence, but what if she ever disagreed or challenged him? She couldn't imagine him ever growing angry, but she'd never believed Senator Rutherford capable of hurting his daughter, either.

Once they'd eaten, he folded the napkin, tucking it under the edge of his plate. "You ready?"

Melanie nodded, feeling excited about spending the day at the carnival with Seth.

He stood and pushed in his chair. "Just to warn you, I hold the town record for Whack-a-Mole. Three years now, undefeated."

"Oh my." A smile grew on Melanie's face. "I didn't realize I was with a celebrity."

Grinning, Seth inclined his head. "Understandable. I *am* very humble about it."

Melanie giggled and shook her head.

They bid Beatrice farewell and joined the crowd moving toward Grant's Park.

As she watched him from the corner of her eye, she noticed how straight he walked, swinging his arms, smiling at passersby. Seth was confident, strong where she was lacking, and she was tempted to lean on his steadiness. Knowing he'd also left behind family expectations to find his own happiness made her feel instantly connected. If only she'd been brave enough to do the same without feeling the need to hide.

Seth would never even consider a marriage for a reason as ludicrous as winning over constituents. She glanced at him, and her cheeks heated when she saw his smile. What kind of marriage *would* Seth consider? And why did the question make her heart beat double-time?

They stopped on First Street and waited for the trolley to pass, and then continued. Melanie smiled as she looked around the town. Lobster Cove residents had been preparing for the holiday for weeks. Flags, banners, and ribbons decorated the shops, and Melanie had heard excited chatter about the different carnival booths, the events, and the culmination of the celebration: a fireworks show over the lake. They reached the park, and music, the sounds of happy shouts, and the clangs and beeps of games filled the air. She smelled baked goods, fried food and barbecue, and saw the townsfolk consuming popsicles, soda, and ice cream to keep cool as they walked between exhibits.

Seth pointed to the Whack-a-Mole booth and opened his mouth to say something when the sound of his name stopped him.

"Dr. Goodwyn!" A young boy ran toward him, a plaster cast holding his arm at a ninety-degree angle. "Will you sign my cast?"

Seth knelt on one knee and took the marker the boy offered. "Hey, Andrew! How's the elbow feeling?" He scribbled his name on a blank space among the mostly child handwriting graffiti covering the cast.

"Hurts a little. But I can still ride my bike." The boy grinned, showing missing teeth.

"But you always wear a helmet, right?" Seth spread his hand over Andrew's hair like he was palming a basketball and shook it the slightest bit. "I can fix elbows, but heads are a lot trickier."

The boy laughed. "Yeah, my mom always makes me."

"Listen to your mom." Seth stood and waved to a woman holding a bag of cotton candy.

"Thanks, Dr. Goodwyn." Andrew rushed back to join his mother.

Heat spread through her chest as Melanie watched

the scene. Seth had been so comfortable and so gentle with the boy, and though the encounter lasted less than a minute, Melanie felt something inside her that she didn't quite understand. The warmth increased when Seth turned and his gaze found hers.

He glanced toward the carnival game, but another child, a girl this time, caught his attention with a shy wave.

The girl was small with her dark hair held back in red, white, and blue ribbons. She held the hand of a man who stood talking with a couple.

Melanie couldn't begin to guess a child's age, but the girl was too young to be a Trawler. Maybe six?

Seth waved back.

The girl turned her face against the man's leg.

Melanie's heart went out to the little girl. She knew exactly the feeling of being too shy to speak.

Seth caught Melanie's gaze and tipped his head toward the Whack-a-Mole booth. As they walked toward it, they passed closely by the little girl.

She peeked from behind the man's leg.

"Hi, Halle," Seth spoke in a soft voice.

"My throat doesn't hurt anymore." Halle's voice was nearly a whisper.

Seth greeted the man, shaking his hand and knelt down until he was eye level with Halle. "Did you take all your medicine?"

She nodded making the ribbons bounce. "All of it. Just like I promised."

"I'm so glad. You wouldn't enjoy the carnival if you were still sick."

"I rode on the Ferris wheel."

"What a lucky girl. Maybe I'll have to try it out."

Halle glanced up at Melanie. "Is she your wife?"

At the words, Melanie felt her heart seize, and she saw the back of Seth's neck turn red.

"This is my friend, Melanie." He motioned for Melanie to join them.

She stood behind Seth, unsure of what to do. Should she kneel?

"Mel, I'd like you to meet one of my favorite patients, Halle."

"Hi, Halle." She waved awkwardly, not having any idea how to talk to a young child. Aside from the Trawlers, she'd seldom had contact with children. Certainly never back home. And with the kids on her team, knowing what to say was easy, she just showed them how to play softball.

Seth rose. "Hope you enjoy the carnival, Halle."

"You, too, Doctor Goodwyn."

Seeing his wink and smile, Melanie realized how much Seth enjoyed what he did. He was comfortable around the people, and he seemed to especially connect with the kids.

Seth will be a good dad. The thought hit her out of the blue and brought her up short. Music played over the speakers, people laughed and called to one another and the whirrs and bleeps of the carnival games sounded around her, but Melanie tuned all of it out, her mind zeroing in on the notion.

He glanced to see why she stopped, raising his brows in a question.

Melanie smiled and continued walking toward the carnival booth. She'd never had such a thought—about anyone. Of course, she'd dated and assumed she'd eventually get married. But most of the guys who she'd gone out with were social climbers, not the type to be thinking about parenthood. Usually not much time passed before a guy mentioned how much he wanted to meet her father, or somehow work into the conversation how beneficial a government internship would be to his career. While the comments could have been nothing more than innocent conversation, she had never been completely sure of the reasons they'd asked her out in the first place.

She'd never considered any of those dates as potential fathers. Why hadn't she? In just the last few minutes, the bar has been raised on future husband qualifications, and the direction her thoughts were taking made her nervous.

Seth approached the Whack-a-Mole booth and handed two bills to the teenage girl behind the counter. "Wanna go first, Mel?"

Flashing a smile, she shook her head. Her mind still spun from her unexpected thoughts. "I came to watch the master."

He twirled the foamy mallet and spread apart his legs. The look in his eyes was one of fierce concentration as he waited for the game to start. Once the moles began popping out of their holes, Seth pounced.

Melanie put her hand over her mouth to hold back a laugh. She didn't want to distract him, or hurt his feelings, but the sight of a grown man so intent on a carnival game was something she'd never witnessed in her life.

His arm was a blur. The faster he moved, the more people stopped to watch. He hit the little mole heads so quickly that there was hardly a pause between "thumps."

When the buzzer went off, a cheer from the bystanders rose.

Seth turned and wiped the back of his arm across his forehead. "Whew!" He bowed for the crowd, and then looked to the digital scoreboard above the game.

"Three ten." The girl took the mallet. "That's the highest score I've seen."

"I have a good luck charm." Grinning, Seth jerked his head toward Melanie.

She knew her cheeks flamed red and wondered what it would be like to possess his level of self assurance.

"You can choose a prize." The girl pointed to a row of stuffed animals hanging along the top of the booth.

"Normally, I only play for the glory." His breath came out in huffs. "You choose, Mel."

She pointed to a penguin. A warm feeling spread through her chest as she thought how similar the bird looked to a puffin.

When Seth took it from the girl, he held it over his head like a victory trophy then presented it to Melanie. "This guy can keep your misguided bear in line. Penguins are Sox fans."

Feeling like a teenager in a movie, Melanie just rolled her eyes. She'd been given gifts by men before, but never a tacky prize from a carnival game. The gift made her feel special in a way she couldn't explain. And she knew it was completely ridiculous. She held the penguin up to her ear. "What's that? Your name is Mariano Riviera?"

Seth threw back his head and groaned. "Oh, you've got to be kidding me."

She laughed, patting the toy's head. "Of course

we're watching the game this weekend. And you'll love your big brother, Jeter."

He groaned again, but the sound was followed by a smile and a wink.

The pair wandered through the carnival, stopping occasionally at a booth to look at the carnival merchandise or to try out a game. They ate ice cream, and Melanie greeted a few of the kids from her team. She knew a few other people from the coffee house and exchanged hellos with them as well. But Seth knew everybody.

A few people stopped him to ask about medical problems they were having. Instead of making an excuse, he listened each time, giving advice or telling them to come into the clinic tomorrow. He smiled as he greeted Lobster Covians old and young, always taking the time to speak with someone. Never acting like he was too busy.

Melanie was reminded of her father when he campaigned—hugging, shaking hands, smiling, waving to everyone he saw. Even kissing babies. But with Seth, his attitude seemed different. And though she didn't know him well, she could tell he wasn't just putting on a show. He actually cared about the people.

After a few hours of wandering, snacking, and greeting neighbors, the two decided to head back to Seth's car for a blanket to save a spot on the grass for the fireworks show.

As they passed through the ride area, Seth pointed to a couple standing beside the temporary metal fence surrounding the carousel. "There're Nathaniel and Val. He's been my best friend since we were kids. Is it ok if we go say hi?"

"Of course." She hoped he couldn't tell that her heart rate had sped up. She fought to keep her breath steady.

"Nathaniel! Val!" Seth called out to his friends.

They turned, and Melanie studied the couple. Nathaniel seemed a bit older than his companion—maybe in his early thirties, like Seth. The woman, Val, had blonde hair and a bright smile. While they were both attractive, she thought the couple seemed mis-matched based on their personal fashion sense. Nathaniel dressed in the same conservative New England-style as Seth while Val had a more eccentric style that Melanie would classify as "cowgirl."

"Val, Nathaniel. I'd like you to meet Melanie Owen." Seth touched the small of Melanie's back, urging her to take a step forward.

Melanie could tell by the way he smiled that their meeting was important to him, but hearing her assumed name reminded her to be on guard. Would either of these two recognize her?

Nathaniel darted a glance at Seth, then shook Melanie's hand. "Nice to meet you."

"Hi, Melanie." Val smiled and offered her hand. "Nice meetin' ya."

Her accent was southern. Maybe the "cowgirl" label wasn't so far off. "Likewise." Melanie shook Val's hand and smiled.

"Been here long?" Seth asked.

"Just arrived." Nathaniel waved at the children on the carousel.

Seth shifted, twisting slightly to include Melanie in their circle. "Mel and I were on our way to set out blankets by the lake. Want us to save you a place for the fireworks?"

"We have a blanket in the car." Nathaniel lifted his chin toward the town center. "I'll grab it and help you save some spots." He turned to Val and raised his brows. "If Val doesn't mind me leaving her with the kids on her day off."

Melanie thought it was a strange thing to say, but she'd had such limited interaction with young families that she wouldn't judge their parenting approach.

Val waved her had in the air. "Course not. Go ahead, and we'll catch up when y'all get back."

Seth touched Melanie's arm and leaned to speak close to her ear. "Will you be okay here with Val and the kids for a minute?"

Melanie nodded. "Sure." She knew her voice was quiet and hoped she didn't sound hesitant. Staying with Val didn't bother her at all. She smiled, hoping Seth wouldn't worry about making her uncomfortable. Inside, she prayed Val wouldn't ask too many questions.

Glancing up, she saw Nathaniel studying her. His expression seemed curious, but she didn't know whether it was because she looked familiar, or if he just wondered about her as Seth's friend. She tipped her head forward to let her hair fall in front of her face and tried for a nonchalant attitude.

She couldn't believe her life had come to a point where she cowered in a corner and hid her face while a calliope played carousel music. *What am I doing?* Melanie'd asked herself the same question all day, and she still had no answer.

Chapter Four

Seth felt Nathaniel's gaze as the two walked down Second Street toward the movie theater parking lot. He knew his friend was curious about Melanie, but Seth wasn't sure exactly what to tell him. *Melanie and I are complicated.* How else could he describe a relationship that began with him breaking into her apartment?

"So Melanie, is it?" Nathaniel finally broke the silence.

"Yep." Seth glanced at him, hoping to see anything in his friend's expression that might give an opinion. "You sound skeptical."

"Curious. I didn't know you were seeing someone. Why haven't you mentioned her?"

Seth blew out a breath. He could think of a hundred reasons he hadn't told Nathaniel about Melanie on their morning runs. He, of course, hadn't known her long. And the only occasion that was even close to a real date was their picnic. But he didn't think those reasons were what kept him from bringing her up. Something about Melanie made him want to keep her and their budding relationship to himself. He wanted to protect her secret, even if he didn't understand her reasons behind it. He also didn't want to answer the myriad of questions Nathaniel was sure to ask. He was an attorney after all. Talking about her felt like a violation of her privacy. And if there was one thing Melanie wanted, it was privacy. "We're not really seeing each other. She's new in town, and we just happened to come to the carnival together."

"Uh huh." Nathaniel cocked a brow.

"What does that mean?" Seth crossed his arms, a mixture of defensiveness and confusion battled within his thoughts And also a little pleasure at knowing Nathaniel might think there was more to the relationship.

Nathaniel shrugged. "Nothing."

They split to walk around a cluster of women.

"How's Val?" Seth said when he rejoined Nathaniel on the path between the carnival booths.

"Changing the subject?"

"Curious." Seth mimicked his friend's earlier statement.

"Val's great. Best nanny I've ever had. The kids adore her, and I don't know how we ever got along without her." Nathaniel gave him a sidelong glance.

The look seemed intended to show just how easy it was to answer a question. "Gonna be rough when she leaves at the end of the summer." Seth knew he was prying, but he wanted to see if he could get any reaction.

Nathaniel stuffed his hands into his pockets and stared straight ahead.

Seth figured his friend's action was an answer in itself.

When they reached the parking lot, Nathaniel clicked his fob, opening the car's trunk. He pulled out a cooler, blankets, sweatshirts, and a backpack, piling the items behind the car.

"Wow." Seth lifted the cooler from the asphalt. "What do you have in here? Bricks?"

Nathaniel grinned. "You know Val's a southern girl. She doesn't mess around when food's involved."

"We should have stopped at my car first. I'll hurt my back carrying all this."

"Just wait until you have kids. You'll be surprised at the amount of stuff you have to bring everywhere."

"Yeah, well don't hold your breath. By the time that happens, *your* kids will be old enough to schlep around this stuff for me." Reverting to his persona of "cocky bachelor" didn't bring the same amusement it typically did. He didn't like thinking too deeply about the path his personal life was on. Over the years, he'd dated nearly every single woman in this small town, and though he pretended to enjoy the reputation of a player, in actuality he was lonely. And the "cocky bachelor" routine was feeling pathetic. He was looking for more.

Once they'd retrieved the items from Seth's car, the men walked to the lake and spread out the blankets on the grassy field.

"If we're lucky, Finn will fall asleep before the night gets too late," Nathaniel said. "Ruby will be fine to stay up, but that little boy turns into a dragon when he's tired."

Seth laughed, feeling the pang of loneliness return. He loved Nathaniel and his kids, but someone else's family was no substitute for his own. He thought of Melanie and the way she cheered for the kids at practice, patiently showing them how to hold a bat and giving each a high five when they came in from the field. The image of her as a mother entered his mind. He couldn't imagine her ever raising her voice in anger. She was gentle and happy and...his thoughts were jerked up short as if someone had poured a bucket of ice water over him. Melanie Owen was obviously not staying in Lobster Cove. And she wasn't even Melanie Owen. Her charade or escape or disguise, or whatever it was, couldn't last forever.

And he couldn't imagine she'd remain once it ended.

As they walked back toward the carnival, he glanced to the side to again find Nathaniel watching him with squinted eyes and a tipped head. He recognized the expression his best friend made when he was trying to figure something out. "Hey, so can I ask you a question?"

"As in an 'I need an attorney' question? Or just a casual, 'I wonder' question?"

"The latter."

"You don't need permission to ask a question."

As they walked to the carnival, the noise increased. Seth rolled his eyes. "Let's say you know someone's secret, but the person doesn't know you know."

"Is the someone Melanie?"

Seth shot him a glare. "We're speaking hypothetically."

Nathaniel smirked, but his eyes were thoughtful. "So, what's the question?"

"Do you wait for the person to tell you on her own? Or do you tell her you know?"

Nathaniel was quiet for a moment. He scratched his cheek. "Do you know why the person is keeping the secret?"

"Not completely. I have some guesses."

"Is the secret hurting anyone? Breaking the law?"

"No." Seth set the cooler on the grass, opening and closing his hands to ease the cramping.

Nathaniel stopped and turned. "Are you afraid revealing what you know might threaten her trust?"

Seth didn't bother pretending they weren't both talking about Melanie. "That's exactly what I'm afraid of."

"But, on the other hand, you think maybe she'd be relieved to know she can talk to someone."

As he lifted the cooler, Seth grunted. "I guess we've moved away from hypothetical," he muttered.

They continued through the crowd. "My advice would be to wait for her to tell you on her own," Nathaniel said.

Seth squinted, looking around the picnic area for Melanie and Val and the kids. "That's my gut instinct, too. It's just...I wish she trusted me."

They walked silently past the rides toward the games. Seth considered Nathaniel's advice. He'd thought the same, but hearing someone he trusted confirm his intuition was refreshing. If only he could figure out how to show Melanie that he understood.

Nathaniel cleared his throat. "Listen, I have to spend some time in the Boston office over the next few weeks. You mind checking on Val and the kids?"

"Course not. Maybe I'll bring Daisy and let them chase her around."

"They'd love that." Nathaniel nodded. He stayed quiet for a moment, and then cleared his throat. "How do the Red Sox look compared to the rest of the division?"

"Bullpen's got to get a little stronger if we're making a push to the playoffs." Seth felt his shoulders relax, relieved they were finally on a neutral topic.

"Starting rotation's looking tight."

An idea that had tickled the back of Seth's mind moved to the forefront. "So, does your firm still have Sox season tickets?"

Nathaniel nodded. "You thinking of seeing a game?"

"Maybe. What are the chances of me taking Melanie next week?"

"The series against the Yankees?" Nathaniel darted a glance at his friend.

Seth shrugged, not sure how to break the news. "Yeah, Mel's…"

Nathaniel's eyes grew wide and he grimaced. "Oh, no. Please don't say she's a Yankee's fan."

"I know. I'm working on it."

"She looks so…nice."

"Careful…" Seth warned, though he knew his friend was teasing. Seth considered himself a loyal Sox fan, but Nathaniel treated the Red Sox practically as a religion.

"I might have to rethink all that fantastic advice I gave you. But this fact just shows that nobody's perfect." He wrinkled his eyes and bared his teeth, as if he was in pain. "Really? A Yankees fan?"

"The tickets…?" Seth reminded him.

Pursing his lips, he nodded, "That series is in high demand, especially since it's Derek Jeter's last season…but I'll see what I can—" Nathaniel broke off, and a grin spread over his face. "There they are." He motioned with his chin toward the shooting gallery.

As they got closer, Seth could tell by the number of downed targets that Val was an expert shot. They waited until the music stopped, signaling her game was finished. "Looks like your nanny's attracting some attention." He motioned to the crowd that had gathered.

Melanie furrowed her brow. She moved to stand beside Seth while Val played again. "Nanny?" She spoke in a low voice.

He leaned down his head to hear her.

"I thought they were married." She lifted her gaze back toward Nathaniel and Val, then to the kids. "They seem so…I don't know, *right*."

He felt the same and liked knowing their perceptions of the couple matched. "They're great together, and everyone can see it but them."

"I hope they figure it out," she nearly whispered. "Losing something so special would be heartbreaking." She darted her gaze to his and back to the other couple. Red bloomed over her cheeks.

His earlier realization crashed over him. Melanie's time in Lobster Cove was temporary. Hollowness ate at his gut. *My thoughts exactly.*

After the fireworks show, Seth and Melanie helped carry sleeping children, blankets, carnival prizes, and a cooler to Nathaniel's car. They bid their friends farewell and walked toward the center of town. Once they reached the main square, most of the crowds had dissipated, and only traffic remained.

Seth turned from the sidewalk, cutting through the park by the Captain's Library. After the noise of the music and crowds, and the bangs of the light show, the night seemed extra quiet with only the whoosh of the waves in the harbor. He relaxed as they strolled beneath the street lamps. In the distance, they could see the flashes of the Bar Harbor fireworks.

"I had fun today, Seth. Thank you." Melanie smiled. "You were right about a small town Fourth."

Though she didn't say anything, her expression made his heart beat speed up. Her smile was soft, but not shy. *Does she feel comfortable with me*? The skin of his arm next to hers heated, even without touching. He took a chance and caught her hand.

Melanie didn't pull away, but she slowed her pace.

Seth matched her speed. "Probably nothing like the celebration in D.C, though."

She shrugged. "I never saw—" Shaking her head, she glanced to the side. "I...we didn't live there all year."

"So where...? Sorry. I don't mean to pry. I just want to know about you."

With her free arm, Melanie hugged the penguin tighter.

Seth felt her tension and knew he'd overstepped. He halted, tugging on her hand and forcing her to stop. "Mel, listen." He waited for her to look at him. Her expression was nervous and he knew what he said now would make or break it. "I know there's stuff you don't want to talk about it. Things that have been rough on you or that you want to get away from. Whatever all that is, none of it matters to me." He raised their joined hands and tapped beneath her chin to keep her from looking down.

"I mean it. You don't have to tell me anything you don't want, and when you're ready, I'm here to help, okay?"

Melanie's eyes shone in the light of the streetlamps. When she blinked, tears escaped in trails down her cheeks. "I'm sorry. You're such a good friend, and it's not that I don't trust you. I just need to figure myself out." She shook her chin away and tucked the penguin under her arm so she could wipe her fingers over her cheeks. "I'm not doing a very good job."

"I understand." Seth tugged at her hand, and they continued their stroll.

"Do you?"

He paused before answering. Did he understand her reasons for keeping her identity a secret? For hiding in Lobster Cove? For living in a crappy one-bedroom apartment over a bar when she'd left behind a mansion? "I'm trying to," he said honestly.

"So am I," Melanie whispered.

****

The next week at the ballpark, Melanie wound up and tossed a pitch.

The batter swung and missed…again.

Across the distance, she saw the girl's eyes fill with tears. "Hey, Lily. You're doing great. Choke up on the bat a little."

Lily wiped her hand across her face and sniffed. She wrinkled her nose and shook her head.

She must not understand the instruction. The girl looked so small with the batting helmet on. The sight made Melanie's stomach tight. She looked over her shoulder at the third base coach. Holding up the ball, she raised her brows. "Can you pitch, Coach Goodwyn?"

Seth jogged to the mound and took her glove, grinning. "You got it, Coach Owen."

Melanie hurried to home plate and stood behind Lily. "You're doing everything right. Hold the bat up here." She helped shift the girl's hands higher. "And don't hesitate. Seeing the ball come toward you can be a little scary, but don't worry. He's a good pitcher. He won't hit you." Seeing Lily's nod, Melanie stepped back.

Seth tossed in a slow pitch.

Lily swung…and connected with a *thwack*. The ball bounced past the shortstop into the outfield. She looked back at Melanie with wide eyes and a grin.

"Run!" Melanie pointed, and then watched Lily drop the bat and dash toward first base. She clapped and cheered with the rest of the team when Lily ran across the plate.

Looking around the field, Melanie felt her heart expand. The Trawlers had improved so much since the first practice four weeks ago that she hardly recognized them as the same kids. She watched Seth directing the right fielder to throw the ball into second base.

He lifted off his cap and shook his head before pulling it back down.

His movement was so natural, but seeing his bicep flex beneath tanned skin and the sun-highlighted tips of his tousled hair made her draw in a shaky breath. *My assistant coach is sexy, that's all there is to it.*

Seth caught her gaze and his lips rose in a half-smile.

Her insides quivered. Melanie felt a flush covering her skin and looked away, glad he couldn't read her mind. Cars had started filling the parking lot. Practice time was over. She blew her whistle and motioned the team in.

"Trawlers, that was our best practice so far. You're all learning to work together as a team, and I can't tell you how good you look out there." She smiled at all the little faces turned toward her. "And I have some news. Next week instead of regular practice, Coach Goodwyn made arrangements for us to play against a team from

Bar Harbor."

"A real game?" Lily asked Seth, her eyebrows winging high.

He nodded. "Yep. You guys are ready for some real competition."

The players cheered and clapped.

Melanie couldn't help but grin. "I'll text your parents the info this week. So, make sure you get extra sleep and eat spaghetti or something like that the night before to give you energy." She put out her hand. "Ok, team. Trawlers on three."

The kids crowded together, stretching their hands into the circle.

"You, too, coach." Melanie motioned with her head for Seth to join them. "One, two, three, TRAWLERS!" The team flung their hands into the air and cheered.

Once the children left, she and Seth gathered the bases and equipment. She held the duffle bag for him to drop in an armload of softballs. "I don't know how I'd do this without you."

Seth pulled back his head and furrowed his brow. "What are you talking about? You could coach this team alone without breaking a sweat."

"Yeah, maybe." She glanced up, feeling suddenly shy. "But I like having you here."

He gave her a long look before speaking. "Thanks, Mel."

Seth's low voice flowed over her like she'd just sunk into a hot tub. She focused on stacking the batting helmets in the equipment bag until her pulse returned to a normal speed. Pulling the zipper closed, she hefted the bag.

Without a word, Seth took it from her and clasped

her hand as they walked toward his car.

When she'd arrived at practice three weeks earlier, balancing the duffle bag on her bike, Seth had insisted on driving her to and from practice. Her first impulse had been to argue for her independence, but his offer had made her feel cherished instead of dominated. And she still wondered which emotion terrified her more.

He put the equipment into the trunk and opened the passenger door.

Melanie muttered "thanks" as she climbed into the car, her mind still turning over and over. Seth's effortless way of taking care of her—even when he knew she didn't need it—created a feeling inside she'd never felt before. But was she giving up the independence she was so hungry for?

Seth started the car and glanced at her as he turned onto the road. "You seem extra thoughtful today. Got a lot on your mind?"

"I guess I do. Sorry."

He shrugged and slipped his hand under hers, lifting it to the center console. He bumped his thumb over her knuckles. "Hey, I was hoping you'd do me a favor."

"Well, it depends." Melanie saw his lips quirk, and knew he had something up his sleeve. The knowledge that she could read his expression sent tingles over her skin. Or maybe knowing he had a surprise brought on her reaction.

"In the glove box is an envelope. Would you take a look at the papers inside?"

Melanie released his hand and retrieved the envelope. Turning it over, she pulled out two Red Sox tickets. Her heart banged, and a giggle fought its way from her mouth when she saw the Yankees were the visiting team. "Seth." Her hands shook as she returned the tickets into the envelope. "Are you asking me to go with you? To *this game*?" She could hear her voice getting higher and louder, but had zero control at this point.

"Yeah. You can see why I need the favor." He flicked his wrist toward the envelope. "*Two* tickets. I don't want to have to waste one."

"Are you serious?" She felt like bouncing in her seat and clapping her hands.

"I'm always serious about baseball." He smirked, his expression at odds with his words.

"I'd love to go. Thank you." The idea of wrapping her arms around him and covering his cheeks with kisses rose in her mind, making her blush.

"Do you think Carlos will give ya the day off? The game's in the afternoon, so we'll have to leave pretty early in the morning."

Again, Melanie slid out the tickets, just to make sure they were real. Beneath the words "Fenway Park," the Sox and Yankees logos were separated by "vs." She ran her fingertip over the symbols, and another thrill shot through her chest. She nodded. "I'm sure Carlos won't mind."

"Well, that solves my problem." He ran a hand across his forehead, mimicking wiping sweat from his brow, and winked. Once he'd shifted the car into Park, he turned toward her.

"These tickets must have been so hard to get. And especially this season. A rivalry game in a small-capacity stadium. Really, Seth. Thank you so much." Her throat constricted and itching built behind her eyes. But at the same time, she couldn't stop smiling like a lunatic.

Seth studied her face. He brushed his knuckles softly over her cheek. "Seeing that smile is worth any effort."

Melanie's heart flipped. She wanted to close her eyes and sigh, but she needed to maintain some dignity. "So, I'll see ya tomorrow morning. One Americano Latte and a blueberry scone?"

He brushed his thumb over her lower lip. "Yep." His voice was husky and his gaze lingered on her mouth.

Does he want to kiss me? The idea both excited and frightened her. Frightened won. She reached for the door handle and heard Seth blow a breath through his teeth as he opened his own door. Cringing, she hoped she hadn't hurt his feelings.

He pulled the duffel bag from the trunk and grinned with a flash of white teeth.

Melanie felt the familiar jolt in her chest that was becoming more comfortable each time. Once they reached the top of the stairs, she unlocked the door.

Seth turned sideways, brushing against her as he set the bag inside before straightening.

He stood so close that she could feel the heat from his body. Melanie couldn't help herself. She leaned forward and slid her arms around his back, leaning against his chest.

Seth let out a breath. He pulled her close and laid his cheek on her head.

The tumble of emotions inside her overwhelmed her, but one thought hovered and wouldn't be ignored. She was lying to Seth, pretending to be someone she was not. Would he ever forgive her? *Why can't I just tell him?* But she knew the answer. Telling him might lead to losing him. The revelation would definitely change everything.

She had to figure out a way to confess the truth and keep Seth from feeling like he'd been deceived. She had to. But for right now, all she wanted was to be held and feel cared for. She tightened her embrace. Because a sick feeling inside warned her it wouldn't last.

Chapter Five

At seven a.m. on game day, Melanie opened her apartment door.

"You've got to be kidding." Seth's mouth quirked as he leaned his shoulder against the doorframe. "I can't take you to Fenway Park wearing that."

Melanie glanced down at her Yankees jersey and then looked pointedly at Seth's Red Sox T-shirt. "I could say the same about you."

Seth pushed off and took a step toward her. "I'm serious. Sox fans can be...uh, let's call it single-minded."

"So can I." She flipped her ponytail as she stepped past him onto the landing. "Now, come on, or we'll be late."

"How can you possibly look so attractive in that thing?" Seth followed her outside.

Melanie pulled her door shut and turned the knob to make sure it locked. She took her time, leaving her back toward Seth while she waited for the burning in her cheeks to subside. A grin pulled at her lips. *Today will be perfect.* And after the game, she planned to tell Seth everything. The drive was close to four hours each way, plenty of time to explain. She was tired of keeping secrets. Especially from a person she'd started to care about. *Maybe even love.* As her face heated again, she pushed away the thought. *Calm down. It's too soon to be*

thinking like that. I've only known him a few months.
She hurried down the stairs ahead of him.

"So, you ready to watch Jeter today?"

"Yep." Melanie couldn't hold back her grin. "You think he's a first ballot Hall of Famer?" she asked

Seth snorted. "Of course he is. He's the best shortstop in the history of the game. Even if he is a Yankee." He settled into his seat, leaning one elbow against the center armrest. "So, how's it you know so much about baseball? And where'd you learn to play? You former MLB?"

She smirked at his teasing words. "No. I played on an intramural softball team in prep school until—" Melanie stopped short, holding her breath as she felt her chest tighten. She'd almost slipped. Slowly, she blew out a puff of air, deciding maybe this was a chance to test out the waters with Seth. Gauge his reaction. "I stopped once my parents found out. They, um, didn't want me to play."

The skin around his eyes tightened, but he gave no other reaction. "Why not? You love it. And I've seen you pitch. You're good."

Melanie folded her arms. She felt both warmed at his understanding and nervous at sharing something so personal. "Playing ball didn't fit with the image they had in mind." She glanced at him, weighing her words. "My mother and father are...particular...about appearances, and they..." She cleared her throat, feeling nervous that she'd already said too much.

"I'm sorry they'd take away something you're so passionate about."

Melanie nodded. "At first, I just did it to rebel. My dad cheers for the Cubs, so I found my own team, the

Yankees. I followed the team obsessively, reading stats, watching games, sleeping with jersey-wearing teddy bears." She worried the conversation was becoming too serious, and bumped his arm with her elbow. "Ya know—crazy Yankee stuff." Seeing his smirk was a relief. "And, you're right. I do love it. Maybe because ball is one thing that's really 'me,' ya know?" She watched his expression, noticing that his brows had pulled together. *What is he thinking?* "I sound ridiculous, don't I?"

"No. I'm glad you had something of your own." He chewed on his lip and glanced sideways. "I'm glad you told me." He slid his hand under hers and squeezed. "You could have chosen *any* team, you know."

She squeezed his hand back. "If I hadn't been cursing out the Yankees' first baseman that night, you wouldn't have broken down my door and…" She turned to look out the window, feeling suddenly shy.

"You're right." He lifted her hand and brushed a kiss over her fingers. "Looks like I owe a debt of gratitude to New York's crappy infield."

Melanie's fingers tingled, and she was grateful to Seth for joking to keep the mood light. She wasn't, however, going to stand for his insult to her team. "How many championships have the Red Sox won in the last twenty years?"

"Ouch. Let's save the trash talk until *after* the game."

Melanie watched out the window as they left the rocky Maine Coast and drove through thick pine forests interspersed with green meadows. Occasionally, they passed a small town with colorful wooden clapboard houses and quaint white churches. Sprawling green farmland grew more scarce as they neared the city, following the Charles River and finally exiting the turnpike. Signs all around announced they were near Fenway Park, and Melanie had to keep from bouncing in her seat in excitement.

Seth found a parking spot and held onto her hand as they joined the crowd heading toward Fenway Park.

Melanie had only seen the iconic brown stadium with its arched doorways and green stairs on television. A thrill ran through her at seeing it in person, like shivers on a cool night. As they got closer, the crowd grew. Barricades blocked the streets, allowing only foot traffic. The air was filled with the smell of game day food, music, and the voices of excited fans.

Seth walked slowly, pointing out the statues of Ted Williams setting his cap on a young fan's head, and Carl Yastrzemski waving his cap before his last "at bat." As they continued around the stadium, they stopped in front of a bronze sculpture depicting the four "teammates." Seth put his arm over her shoulder, leaning closer to speak above the noise of the crowd. "Ted Williams, Bobby Doer, Johnny Pesky and Dom DiMaggio." He pointed to each of the players on the pedestal. "They all played together before serving in World War II."

Melanie watched his face as he spoke and saw a combination of excitement and reverence in his expression. She loved being with someone who appreciated the game as much as she did.

"Hey, Mac!" A man on the other side of the statue walked toward them looking like an advertisement for the team store.

Seth's arm tightened slightly.

"Why don'tcha get your girlfriend a new shirt?"

Melanie watched the stranger's face, wondering if he was serious. She glanced at Seth's face and saw his jaw was tight.

After a brief hesitation, he smiled but didn't relax. "I'm working on it. Hoping today's game will convince her."

The man's expression didn't soften. He scowled and opened his mouth to say something Melanie was certain she didn't want to hear.

"What do ya think about the third baseman getting scratched from the line-up? My girlfriend thinks they'll have to adjust the entire batting order."

Girlfriend? Seth used the word so casually that she was taken aback.

"Yeah." The man rubbed his chin. "That's a lot of lefties in the line-up."

"Here's hoping the game doesn't have to go extra innings." Seth led her away without waiting for the man to respond. "I told ya, Sox fans can be pretty loyal," he leaned close and whispered in her ear.

Melanie hated to admit it, but she loved that he'd protected her. The sensation of Seth's arm around her shoulders and the knowledge he'd keep her safe made her feel like there was nowhere else she'd rather be. Which was saying something based on her actual location.

Once they entered the stadium, the crush of people made seeing where she was going nearly impossible. She let Seth lead her through the halls and listened as he showed her the array of pictures and pennants. They stepped through an archway into the stands.

Seth pointed toward the famous "red seat" in the right field bleachers. "That's where Ted Williams hit the longest homerun in Fenway history. And you recognize that wall, right? The Green Monster. If ya want, we can go rub it, and give the team luck."

"They're going to need it," Melanie teased. She loved watching the excitement in his face and felt like she was getting to know a new part of Seth. And if the Boston Red Sox was the cause, she'd maybe hate them a little less.

"Too bad it's such an early game, or I'd have brought ya on a tour, showed ya the press box and the trophy hall."

"Maybe next time." Melanie darted a look at him after she said the words, just now realizing the implication behind them. Would there be a next time? Did she and Seth have a future together? He seemed to realize the same thing and his face lit up. His perfect smile lifted his perfect lips, and his eyes sparkled with delight and something more. Something that made Melanie's breath hitch. She looked away quickly as heat rolled up her neck.

"Over there's Pesky's Pole." Seth indicated the right field foul pole.

She'd heard the story of Johnny Pesky winning a game with a homerun hit down the short right field line, right around the pole. Melanie saw a smirk still remained on Seth's lips and wondered if he could tell her heart was turning somersaults.

He squinted. "Our seats are that way, in the field box behind home plate."

Melanie made a move to start down the stairs.

Seth tugged on her arm. "But first, we need to get you a Fenway Frank."

"A hot dog?" She grimaced. "I don't really—"

"Hot dog? Don't insult me." He slapped a hand over his heart. "I'm talking about the best frank you'll ever eat." He slipped his arm around her shoulders, leading her back through the arch to the concessions.

Once they reached the front of the line, Melanie saw the pink dogs rotating behind the glass, and worse, she smelled them. "Um, maybe I'll just get some fries."

"You'll have to try a bite, okay?" He zig-zagged mustard over the dog and covered it with onions.

At the sight, she wrinkled her nose. "We'll see." Hotdogs were pretty far down the list of foods Melanie could stomach.

Once they had their order, the pair headed down the stairs careful not to spill their drinks and muttering apologies as they slid past other spectators, and finally settled into their seats.

"You ready for your frank?" Seth moved the smelly hotdog toward her.

Melanie grimaced and glanced at him. As terrible as it smelled, she didn't want to hurt his feelings, plus she figured a Fenway Frank was part of the experience. She scraped away the onions from one end with her finger and bit into the frank, feeling the hot juice burst through the skin. She smiled at Seth as she chewed, hoping he wouldn't try to get her to eat more. One bite was enough.

"What did I tell ya?" Seth wiped mustard from the corner of her mouth with a napkin."

Melanie took a drink, hoping to get the taste out of her mouth. "It's good."

"You are a terrible liar."

She darted her gaze to him. The words made a bit of guilt churn in her stomach, mixed with processed meat and mustard. Today, she would tell him everything.

Seth took a huge bite of the frank and elbowed her, pointing toward a familiar figure taking the field to warm up.

Derek Jeter. Melanie cheered for her favorite player, earning a few scowls from spectators seated nearby, but she didn't care one bit.

As she gazed out at the ballpark, admiring the white lines and green grass, a thrill went through her, the excitement making her either want to laugh or cry or yell again. She knew she was displaying a dopey grin. She leaned over the armrest and kissed Seth's cheek. "I love this."

His brows rose. "And I thought this day couldn't get any better." He balanced his drink between his legs and laid his arm across the back of her seat.

"You must have forgotten we'll be watching one of the best games of the year." Melanie slid closer, nestling beneath his shoulder. When she glanced up, she saw he was watching her with the same look in his eyes. The one that made her insides turn into jelly.

"As a matter of fact, I did."

****

As he drove toward Lobster Cove, Seth used sideways glances to watch Melanie chatter about the game. Her eyes were bright and her voice animated. He wouldn't have believed a day at the ballpark watching the Sox could be improved on, but today, he'd been proven wrong. The outing had been more perfect than he could have imagined. He smiled as he thought of Melanie's wrinkled nose when she'd taken a bite of his Frank, and his smile grew when he remembered her yelling at the umpire.

Seth's thoughts became more somber as he considered her. What was Melanie's plan? Were her feelings for him deepening in the same way as his own? The idea of her leaving made his chest feel empty. He could still feel a burning on his cheek where she'd kissed him. Not like he'd never been kissed before, and rarely in such a chaste way, but for some reason, her impulsive gesture and the resulting flip of his stomach hadn't left his mind for the rest of the day. *I'm falling for her.* The thought hit him so strongly that he glanced toward Melanie, sure she'd notice some kind of reaction.

"Coach pulled the starter back into the bullpen too early. If he hadn't, Yankees would have won easily. Did you even see their batting streak today? Unbelievable."

Her words brought his mind back from its wandering. Melanie didn't seem too upset about the Yankees loss, but she wanted to discuss the game from every angle. Seth was happy to oblige. "True. The lefty just didn't have his stuff together today. But the errors in the outfield were what cost them the game."

She tapped her finger on her lip. "Sox had the home field advantage, so I guess we wait until tomorrow to see which team's the winner of the series."

"You recording the game so you can scream at the TV alone in the middle of the night?" Seth bumped her with his arm.

Melanie shrugged. A pink blush spread over her cheeks. "Depends on how late I work."

"If you want to watch with us, Daisy and I would love you to come for dinner." He glanced her way and saw the blush had deepened. "We won't even tease when the Sox win."

She grew quiet and rubbed her arms as she turned

her gaze out the window.

The air felt heavy, and Seth got the feeling she had something important to say.

"Seth?" She opened her mouth, and then started to turn, but something caught her gaze and she squinted, bending forward her neck to look out the windshield. "Those dark clouds came in quickly. Do you think they're near home?"

Seth kept his face impassive as he considered her words. Did Melanie consider Lobster Cove home? He squinted and looked at the sky where she indicated. A storm was forecast for tonight, but the cloud mass looked like it was coming in early. He turned on the radio.

The news report confirmed his worry. Heavy winds were already hitting the coast of Maine, and a North Atlantic Storm was on the way.

Seth drummed his fingers on the wheel. He squinted, calculating how quickly he could get home. They were still half an hour away from Lobster Cove, but by the time he drove into town to drop off Melanie, the trip would be closer to an hour before he got home. That is, if no debris blew over the forest roads. Moving branches would only delay him further.

Melanie brushed her fingers over his arm. "You're worried about the storm, aren't you?"

"Yeah. I didn't think it would hit this early. And storms up here are insane." He smiled, hoping to reassure her.

"Will your house be okay?"

He nodded. "Once I fasten the shutters." He mentally kicked himself for not shuttering the windows this morning. In his excitement to get to the game, he'd forgotten.

Squinting, Melanie studied his face. "But you're still worried. Is it Daisy?"

"Storms terrify her." That was the understatement of the century. Last time Daisy had been left alone during a storm, she'd run away and hidden in the forest, and Seth had searched for hours.

As if to emphasize his fears, a gust of wind pushed the car. Seth straightened out the wheel and sped up.

"Let's go to your house first, then. Get things taken care of there."

"Do you mind?" The trees on the side of the road whipped back and forth.

"Of course not." She looked out the window at the choppy ocean.

He threaded his fingers through hers on the center console. Though she acted calm, he could feel that she was tense. "Thanks. Shouldn't take long to batten down the hatches." He tried to keep his voice light.

"No problem." Melanie squeezed his hand.

"Oh, and I promised Nathaniel I'd check on Val and the kids." He placed a quick call. Luckily, Nathaniel had returned home. One less thing to worry about. "Make sure you have flashlights and batteries," Seth told Val before disconnecting.

As he drove up the cliff road, Seth felt his jaw tighten. The heavy black clouds were nearly on top of them. Waves crashed beneath the road. He turned onto the gravel road between the trees. Even inside the car, he could hear the wind wailing and branches snapping.

Melanie's fingers tightened.

Raindrops splattered the windshield just as the car turned from the forest road, past the old wooden fence, and down Seth's lane.

He peered through the storm as they emerged from the trees. Branches wheeled across the yard, but the house seemed undamaged. Once he pulled the car into the garage, he grabbed the flashlight from the glove box, then jumped out and ran to find Daisy. When he reached her chain, he followed it and lifted the end. Her collar was still attached, but the dog was nowhere to be seen. Seth's stomach dropped. "Daisy!" He yelled, but the wind whipped away his words.

"Daisy!" Melanie yelled as she reached him.

Seth hadn't realized she'd followed him. Her wet hair stuck to her face. He grabbed onto her arm, leading her to the porch. "I'll find her. Wait inside."

Melanie shook her head. "You can't do both," she yelled over the wind. "I'll find her while you fasten the shutters. Where do you think she is?"

His insides turned to ice at the suggestion. Splintering branches, lightning, and mud would make the forest into a danger zone. No way would he let Melanie in there. He shook his head. "I got it. You wait inside."

Melanie lifted her chin, and she drew together her brows in a look of determination.

Seth realized what he'd done, and now that he knew more about her past, he understood why his words hurt. He was treating her the very way she resented, taking away her independence, telling her she couldn't handle something. He knew Melanie needed to feel strong, but letting her go when she could get hurt...The acid that burned in his stomach whenever he allowed himself to think of that day with Cassie returned. His heart beat in his ears, and he felt himself shaking. He couldn't do it.

Not when he could keep her safe.

"Seth…" Melanie's lips pursed together defiantly.

"Daisy hides in the forest." He pushed out the words and jerked his head toward the road they'd just traveled. His heart felt like it was being squeezed, but deep down, he knew she needed to do this. "She won't come when you call, so you'll have to search." His throat grew tight as he looked at Melanie. She wore a sweatshirt, but was already soaked through and shivering. She looked so small and fragile. If only…

With a shake of her head, she grasped his hand. "I'm not Cassie."

Seth couldn't do more than nod. He held up the flashlight.

Melanie took it, her expression tightened and worry entered her eyes. But the look was accompanied by a confidence he'd only seen in her when she talked about baseball. She needed this. Needed someone to believe in her.

His fists clenched and his chest feeling hollow, Seth stood in the rain as he watched Melanie disappear into the dark forest. His throat was so tight he had to force himself to swallow. The thing Melanie needed most proved to be one of the hardest things he had ever done.

Chapter Six

Melanie stumbled through the trees. The flashlight only lit a small area, and with the rain and blowing branches, the wet ground seemed to shift. Pine needles hid rocks and holes, and even though she wanted to hurry, she placed each step carefully. "Daisy!" A crash sounded, and Melanie jerked back, slipping in the mud and sitting...hard.

She kept hold of the flashlight and stood, plunging forward. She'd decided if she maintained the same trajectory, following parallel to the road, she could find her way back, but with the whipping wind and rain, she wasn't sure of her direction. "Daisy!" She didn't think yelling did any good, but doing so kept her from feeling completely powerless, and so she kept at it.

As she tripped over branches and pushed her way through undergrowth, she couldn't keep her mind from turning to Seth. Something had happened as they'd stood in the rain. Seth's jaw had been set in a stubborn "no," when she'd offered to find Daisy. She'd fully expected him to pull out the "macho man" act and keep her inside the house like a damsel in distress. According to his body language, he'd wanted to.

But she'd seen fear in his eyes and at that moment, everything shifted once she realized why. Seth had felt helpless and afraid. Just as he'd explained earlier. His need to save people, to keep them safe stemmed from that horrible day so many years ago. And yet...he'd let her go.

Melanie felt tears pressing on the backs of her eyelids and choked on her breath. Seth knew her—he understood, and to him her need had been more important than his own. *I love him.* The thought filled her with warmth like hot cocoa.

A gust of wind thrust her into a tree and Melanie threw up her hands to keep branches from hitting her face. She leaned against the trunk and shined the light through the undergrowth. "Daisy!"

Hearing no doggy sounds, she pushed off and continued forward. After all her whining about the Yankee's coach not having a tight game plan, she was frustrated with herself that she still didn't have any idea of her own life's course. The one thing she felt sure about was Seth. She couldn't imagine a future that didn't include him. Especially after today. Under the wet and cold, she felt warm. Whatever happened, having him in her corner felt good.

She heard a crash and swung around the beam of light. A branch fell from above and landed on a clump of shrubs. "Daisy!" Melanie decided she'd have to change directions or navigate over the broken branch and undergrowth. She decided on a path that would hopefully bring her to the main road and moved around a tree, holding onto a thick branch as she slipped on a wet exposed root. Lightning lit the sky, casting strange shadows and thunder shook the forest. How long had she been gone? Twenty minutes? Thirty? Would Seth come after her if she didn't return soon? She had no doubt he would.

Something knocked into her leg, and Melanie

jumped back. When she caught her balance, she shined the light and saw a trembling mass of wet fur. *Daisy*. Melanie knelt in the mud, examining the dog as well as she could in the rain. The animal looked unhurt. Just wet and frightened. "It's okay, girl. Let's get you home," she spoke in a sing-song voice that she hoped was comforting.

Since Daisy didn't have a collar to hold onto, Melanie walked a few feet and turned, hoping the dog would follow. She didn't have to worry. Daisy stuck close to her side, and Melanie reached down to pat her for reassurance as they made their way through the trees in the direction she hoped led back to the road. A moment later, she emerged onto the gravel drive. "Come on, girl!" she coaxed as she hurried toward the house.

When she emerged into the yard, she saw Seth standing in front of the house. He held his hands over his eyes to block the rain as he scanned the tree line. Melanie knew the instant he saw them.

Seth broke into a run and didn't stop until he'd swept her into his arms and pressed his lips against hers.

The desperation in his kiss surprised her. Melanie could feel his heart pounding and his arms were tight around her. He'd worried about her, and knowing that he'd still let her go against his own convictions sent a warmth through her. Seth made her feel cherished, but he still understood her need for independence.

He pulled away and rested his forehead against hers, his hand cupping the back of her head. His breathing was uneven, and his hands shook. "You're not hurt, Mel?"

Melanie's chest felt tight as she realized the full effect her desire to prove herself had on him. "We're okay," she muttered and placed her hand on his cheeks. "I'm sorry you were worried."

Seth pressed his hand over hers and nodded. He put an arm around her shoulder and glanced down at Daisy who sat in the gravel watching them. "Good girl, Daisy." He snapped his fingers for the dog to follow.

Once they were inside, Seth grabbed a towel and threw it over the dog before she could shake. He handed another to Melanie, glancing down at the mud on her clothes. "You're going to want to shower."

Melanie wiped off her face, glad for the chance to hide behind the towel. Being in Seth's house while the elements raged outside felt so cozy, especially after their kiss. She felt vulnerable standing in a man's living room soaking wet.

After walking away, Seth flipped on a light and called over his shoulder. "Here's the guest room, bathroom's in there. I'll find ya some dry clothes while you shower."

"Thanks." A crash of thunder shook the house and she jumped.

Seth stood in the doorway as Melanie walked into the bedroom. "Nathaniel stayed here a few times when he visited, and my parents once, but this guestroom hasn't gotten much use."

Melanie nodded. Seth seemed to be talking just to fill the silence. She wondered if he felt as nervous as she did with the intimacy of their situation.

"Well, I'll leave you to it..." He closed the door.

Once Melanie had showered, she peeked back into the bedroom and saw a pair of men's plaid pajamas and a long-sleeved Red Sox T-shirt. After she cinched the pajama pants waist and rolled up the cuffs, she lifted the shirt. Glancing at her muddy jersey and sweatshirt, she realized she had no other choice. Which, she was certain, was Seth's evil scheme in the first place.

She entered the living room, and Daisy was the only one on the couch, sitting on a spread towel. The sound of water running told her Seth had waited for her to finish her shower before taking his own. She sat next to the dog and had just started to scratch her ears when the room plunged into darkness.

Daisy whined.

Melanie froze, her pulse racing. *Where is that flashlight?* A burst of lightning and a crack of thunder sounded, making both she and the dog jump. The wind howled and something crashed against the house. She let out a gasp.

"Mel?"

A flashlight beam shined in the hall. "I'm here, in the living room."

"You okay?" He joined her, pushing the dog off the couch and tossing down the wet towel.

"I've never experienced a storm like this." She could hear her voice shaking and felt embarrassed that something as harmless as a rainstorm would scare her so badly.

Seth pulled her against him, leaning back on the couch. He dragged a blanket from the arm rest over them.

Melanie nestled into the space beneath his shoulder, feeling warm and protected. Seth smelled like shampoo and his shirt was damp. He must have jumped out of the shower as soon as the power went off and hurried to find her.

Daisy whined from her spot on the floor.

"Sorry, girl."

Another crack sounded as the wind blew something against the house.

Melanie jumped again and then felt Seth's arms tighten around her. "I'm being such a baby," she said.

"Shhh..." He combed his fingers through her wet hair. "I like taking care of you."

"I like it, too." The crash of the water in the harbor and the noise of the storm grew more distant, and Melanie could feel herself slipping into sleep. Images floated in and out of her thoughts: a mustard-covered hot dog, Seth's white grin, his lips on hers, the muddy dog, the brass plaque by the front door. A feeling of contentment covered her like the blanket. Being held in Seth's arms while the storm raged made her feel safer than any time she could remember. Hyne House felt like home.

****

Melanie squinted at the sunlight on her face. She opened one eye and saw a small beam had made its way between a crack in the shutters. The memory of the night before returned, and she lifted her head. Seth's slow breathing made his chest rise and fall beneath her hand. *Is anything more perfect than waking up like this?* She rose on her elbow to where she could see his face and brushed a kiss on his cheek.

Daisy whined and scratched the back door.

Melanie maneuvered herself over a sleeping Seth and padded across the dimly lit living room. She glanced at the clock. *Still a few hours before I need to get to work.* Then she opened the door, surprised at the brightness of the morning. No trace of last night's storm remained, except for the tree branches and other debris strewn over the lawn. She wasn't sure whether to allow the dog to stay outside alone, but she didn't want to wake Seth to ask, so she closed the door quietly and walked out onto the porch.

Sunlight glinted on the water. Seth's boat bobbed next to the pier, and the sight of the cozy harbor made her heart full. She ran her hand along the railing as she walked barefoot along the back porch. The furniture had been blown into one corner of the deck. She grabbed a chair and dragged it back into place, and then moved another.

"Mornin', sunshine." Seth stood in the doorway, scratching his head sleepily. "What are ya doing out here so early?"

"Good morning." Melanie wrapped her arms around him and felt him press a kiss into her hair. "I let Daisy out." She stepped back and motioned toward the yard.

Seth's mouth spread in a grin. "Nice shirt." He folded an arm across his chest and held his chin, nodding his head. "I forgot all about it in the dark last night. We might need to get one in your size, however."

She glanced down at the Red Sox shirt and rolled her eyes. "Surely, this isn't the only shirt you could have lent me."

His grin grew and he shrugged. "I think we should make a wager on tonight's game. Loser has to wear the other team's jersey to work?"

"You got yourself a deal." Grinning, she held out a hand to shake.

He grabbed it and tugged, catching her and planting a kiss on her mouth. "Deal."

Melanie's clothes were still wet and muddy, but her shoes were dry, so she wore them with Seth's pajamas.

When they went to get in the car, they discovered a tree had blown across the lane and would take a chainsaw to remove.

Seth surveyed the damage with his hands in his pockets. "I'll take ya in the boat."

"Let me hurry and call Carlos." Luckily, her phone still had a bit of charge.

Her boss picked up on the first ring. "Sang Freud Coffee House."

"Morning, Carlos."

"Melanie! Well, if it isn't the local celebrity. I saw the picture of you and Dr. Goodwyn in the paper.

Picture? Her heart thudded. "Oh. I didn't know."

"Pretty adorable, you two—rival baseball fans sharing a hot dog." Headline was something like, 'Love Knows No Team Loyalty.'"

Melanie felt a rush of embarrassment flushing over her skin and turned away from where Seth was dragging tree limbs, glad he couldn't hear what Carlos said.

"There's a tree blocking the road out here." The embarrassment grew when she realized what Carlos would assume at her spending the night at Seth's. "I'll be a little late today."

"No problem."

She could hear the smile in Carlos's voice but didn't want to give him any more to react to. "Bye."

"See ya when you get here."

An hour later, Seth helped her out of the motor boat and onto the Lobster Cove Pier.

Melanie was glad the majority of citizens seemed too busy cleaning up the mess from the storm to look at her outfit of oversized men's pajamas too closely. She'd fallen asleep with wet hair, and now she was certain her lack of make-up wasn't doing her complexion any favors.

Seth held her hand as they walked past the seafood market, up Oak Avenue toward her apartment. The street was nearly empty, probably due to the storm. Only one car was parked in front of Murphy's.

"I'm on shift until five, but how about I pick you up after and we'll catch the game?"

"We should figure out what size shirt you need. I should probably order it now, so you can wear it next week." Melanie smiled as she teased him. From the corner of her eye, she saw a car door open, and a couple stepped out. When her mind registered who it was, Melanie froze.

Senator Rutherford and her mother walked toward them, trailed by a bodyguard and Chuck, the campaign manager.

Panic emptied Melanie's mind. She wanted to run, or hide. Her gaze darted around, and she felt her breath come in bursts.

Seth squeezed her hand.

"Seth…It's my parents. My dad, he's—"

"Mel, I know."

Emitting a gasp, she snapped her head around. "You know?"

"Yeah, I've known for a while. And you got this, Mel."

"I can't." She looked at him, then at her approaching parents. Her mind spun as she vacillated between dread, surprise, and the resolve to stand her ground. "I need you."

"You don't need me. You can handle this."

She shook her head, and then held his gaze. Her

throat went dry and she pressed a hand to her jumpy stomach. "I want to need you, Seth." Making the admission was frightening, but once she said it, she knew it was true.

His mouth opened, and then closed. He swallowed hard and pulled her under his arm for a quick hug. "Then I'm here." He lowered his arm.

Melanie clasped his hand.

"Melanie Rutherford." Her father stormed close and stopped. His face was red beneath his thick silver hair, and veins bulged at his neck. "We have been searching for you for months, and we find you in this backwoods town, working as a *waitress*." He rubbed a spot on his forehead. "What on earth are you doing? Do you have any idea what people would think if they knew?" His gaze traveled over her disheveled clothing and moved to Seth. "Who is this *person*?"

Melanie's mother stood behind her father.

Hearing the dismissal in her father's words made Melanie cringe. Especially as they related to Seth. "I'd like you to meet Dr. Seth Goodwyn." She moved her hand, palm up between the men. "Seth, this is my father, Senator Martin Rutherford. And my mother, Mrs. Donna Rutherford."

The senator's lip curled at Seth's attempt to shake his hand. "What do you mean by this, young lady? You've caused us quite a lot of work with your little stunt."

Melanie winced at his tone but felt strength from Seth beside her. "I wasn't happy with the path my life was on," she said slowly. "I know I behaved poorly, but I didn't know what else to do."

Her mother stepped forward, her stilettos clacking

on the pavement. "But honey, running away?"

Senator Rutherford blew out a breath and shook his head dismissively. "Your life was on a fine path, and with a little work, we can cover this up and get you back to where—"

"No." The volume of Melanie's voice surprised even herself. "I'm an adult, and I want to make my own choices." She glanced at Seth and saw his nod. The small movement boosted her confidence even higher. "I've made a life for myself here."

"This isn't what your mother and I want for you, Melanie." Her father folded his arms.

"What about what *I* want for me?" Her throat tightened, and she fought against the shaking in her voice. "I don't want to marry Graham Stewart." She felt Seth tense. "I don't want to work for your charities or make every single decision in my life based on pleasing your voters."

Senator Rutherford's impassive expression seemed frustrated and bored at the same time. "Then what do you want?"

Melanie squared her shoulders. "I want to stay here and coach my softball team and be a member of this community. I don't know what I'll end up doing, but I want to find it out on my own."

Her father snorted. "You can't be serious. Young lady, I've had about enough of this. It's already been a long day. I had to take a flight first thing this morning to Maine of all places and find my daughter parading through town wearing a man's pajamas. Your decisions are poor. You don't know what you want. Now, get in the car. Graham is still willing to take you back, but you need to stop these stunts." He flipped his hand in the air.

"I'm not leaving." Melanie fought to keep her voice calm, even though she felt furious her father hadn't taken her declarations seriously.

"Melanie Rutherford," her father spoke quietly. "I am in a position to shut down a particular coffee shop for tax evasion when I inform the IRS Carlos Young apparently hired a woman under a false name. I can make sure that Dr. Goodwyn never works in medicine again, and I can certainly take your name off any trusts and bank accounts."

Her father's low, icy-calm voice sent a chill over her skin.

Her mother's eyes were wide as she watched her husband. She smoothed her thick hair with a shaky hand.

Melanie's stomach felt like it held a boulder. *My father would blackmail me?* Her muscles tightened and her breathing turned raspy. She eyed the bodyguard and the campaign manager. Her dad wouldn't tell them to grab her and throw her into the car, would he? She didn't know what he was capable of. She'd seen his angry reaction when she'd refused to date Graham. But those were just words. How much more vicious could he become now that she'd taken action?

She squeezed Seth's hand, feeling tears leak out of her eyes in spite of her efforts to quell them. "I'm not leaving," she repeated. "But I'm not hiding anymore, either."

"Melanie," her mother reached out her arm, wiggling her fingers as if she wanted to lead her daughter away from all this. "Come on home, dear."

"Mother, Father." Melanie straightened her shoulders. "I want to be part of your lives. But I want my own life, too."

"We've given you your…" her father began, puffing out his chest.

"Not the life you made. The life *I* make." She wondered if anyone besides Seth knew she was trembling.

"What's your plan, Melanie?"

The entire group turned as Chuck spoke.

"I'm not completely sure." She felt a nervous quiver in her stomach. "I'm coaching a softball team, and I love it." She glanced at her parents, hoping to see a look of approval in their expressions. At least they finally looked like they were paying attention to what she said. "And I thought maybe the Rec program here could be expanded. I like working with kids."

"This could work, Rutherford," Chuck paced, nodding as he spoke. "Good publicity, your daughter living in a small town, working with the community. Her new direction could be a great asset to your campaign."

The senator looked at his campaign manager and then his daughter.

Melanie held his gaze, even though every bit of her wanted to pull away.

Folding his arms, Melanie's father turned to Seth, studying him with a raised chin and narrowed eyes. "And what are your intentions with my daughter, doctor?"

"Seth." He smiled at Melanie. "I love her, sir. I hope to be part of her life for as long as she'll let me."

Melanie's mother pressed her hands to her mouth. "Oh, my dear." She pulled Melanie into an embrace, and then did the same with Seth.

Melanie had rarely been hugged by her mother and was surprised by how much she wanted a warm relationship with her parents.

Senator Rutherford maintained his thoughtful expression. Finally, he dipped his head in a nod. "See that you take care of her."

"She doesn't need taking care of, sir." Seth held the senator's gaze.

Melanie's father studied Seth for a moment longer, and then turned back toward the car. "When she's changed, get some pictures, Chuck."

Chuck caught Melanie's eye and winked.

****

That afternoon, Seth pulled the clinic's glass door closed behind him. He walked across the parking lot and crossed the street toward Murphy's Bar. Raising his gaze to Melanie's window, he felt his heart speed up, and he walked faster.

When he reached the apartment door, he heard the pre-game show on the TV and grinned. He knocked.

Moments later, Melanie opened the door and stepped aside to let him in. "Did you mean what you said to my father, Seth?"

Her brow was furrowed, and he could tell she'd been thinking about the encounter with her parents that morning. "Which part?"

"All the parts."

Seth pulled her toward him, holding her chin with one hand and the other went around her waist. "I meant it when I said I wanted to be part of your life."

Her expression didn't fully relax. "What about the other part?"

"That you don't need to be taken care of?" He slid

his hand beneath her ear, drawing her closer for a kiss.

She moved her hands up his back, tightening her arms around him as she returned the kiss. She pulled back. "And...?" The lines between her brows deepened.

Seth fought to keep a straight face. He knew exactly what she was asking, and also that she was too embarrassed to ask outright. Her uncertainty and the wide-eyed concern in her expression were completely adorable, and he decided to make her sweat it out a bit longer. "Let me see, I actually don't remember much more. Your father is really intimidating."

He moved toward the couch. "Since the game's just about to start, should we watch here?" Plopping down, he picked up the two stuffed animals. "Hey, Jeter. Mariano." He could see from the corner of his eye that Melanie hadn't moved, and he held in his smile. He was enjoying himself. "So, Mel, did you happen to bring any blueberry scones from the coffee house today?"

Melanie sat on the edge of the couch and tucked her hair behind her ear.

Seth saw the shy woman he'd been attracted to months ago, but now he knew beneath her quiet exterior was a warrior. He couldn't be more proud. Finally, he caved. "Are you wondering about the part where I said I love you?"

Melanie lifted her gaze and her cheeks flushed red.

He would never grow tired of bringing color to her cheeks.

"Do you?" She looked back down at her fingers.

She spoke in a soft voice that made his heart flip over. He scooted across the space and pulled her up onto his lap. His somersaulting heart picked up speed. "Mel, I know you want to be on your own. And I don't want to make it harder, but I'm in love with you."

Melanie sank against him. "I wanted to be on my own, but it doesn't mean I have to do it alone, right?"

"I was hoping you'd say that."

Putting her hands on his shoulders, she pulled back. "I love you, Seth."

Hearing the words out loud sent heat spreading through his chest. "Even if I'm a Red Sox fan?"

"Well...I could probably overlook that one flaw." Her lips twisted into a smirk. Leaning forward, she pressed a tentative kiss to his lips, and then did it again.

He pulled her closer, deepening the kiss and smiling at the sound of her sigh. He'd burst through Melanie's door determined to save her, but she hadn't needed a protector, which is why her admission of wanting him made him feel so much more heroic. He wondered if she realized it. Or if his reasoning even made sense. But he figured they had forever to discuss it. Her lips moved over his, and talking was the farthest thing from his mind.

A word about the author...

Jennifer Moore is a passionate reader and writer of all things romance due to the need to balance the rest of her world that includes a perpetually traveling husband and four active sons, who create heaps of laundry that is anything but romantic.

She suffers from an unhealthy addiction to eighteenth- and nineteenth-century military history and literature, and she thinks a man nothing without regimentals.

Jennifer has a B.A. in Linguistics from the University of Utah and is a Guitar Hero champion.

She loves studying maps and traveling, and tries to convince her husband that researching the history of a destination is nearly as fun as actually being there. Her very favorite places to visit are Southern Spain and Greece.

Jennifer spends an excessive amount of time driving carpools and attending kids' soccer games.

She lives in northern Utah with her family, but most of the time wishes she were on board a frigate during the Age of Sail.

http://www.authorjmoore.com

~

Other Titles by this Author
Change of Heart
The Sheik's Ruby

Thank you for purchasing
this publication of The Wild Rose Press, Inc.

If you enjoyed the story, we would appreciate your
letting others know by leaving a review.

For other wonderful stories,
please visit our on-line bookstore at
www.thewildrosepress.com.

For questions or more information
contact us at
info@thewildrosepress.com.

The Wild Rose Press, Inc.
www.thewildrosepress.com

Stay current with The Wild Rose Press, Inc.

Like us on Facebook

https://www.facebook.com/TheWildRosePress

And Follow us on Twitter
https://twitter.com/WildRosePress